Yam Hill

Handersen Publishing, LLC
Lincoln, Nebraska

Yam Hill

Manufactured in the United States of America.

Summary: After the Great Unexpected Tragedy decimates the world's population, the few survivors are forced to live inside a mountain-sized potato in northern Idaho.

Library of Congress Control Number: 2016919271
Handersen Publishing, LLC, Lincoln, Nebraska
ISBN-13: 9781941429600
ISBN 10: 1941429602

Publisher Website: www.handersenpublishing.com
Publisher Email: editors@handersenpublishing.com

For Bossman

Yam Hill

Tevin Hansen

Handersen Publishing LLC
Lincoln, Nebraska

Yam Hill

I

In the future, everyone's skin will be the same color. Orange.

There will be different shades of orange, some darker, some lighter, but nonetheless orange. There will be no more pumpkins. No oranges. No orange juice.

Only yams.

2

When Polly woke up, breakfast was already on the table. Scrambled yams for breakfast, cold yams for lunch, boiled yams for dinner. This was the typical diet of every inhabitant of Yam Hill.

Sometimes families would switch things around. Boiled yams for breakfast, sliced yams for lunch, and maybe cold mashed yams for supper.

Cooking was common inside Yam Hill, but a nuisance. The time involved to properly cook a meal, using the supplied wire and metal clips, could take hours, or even a day or more. That's why most people opted for cold or room temperature yams.

"Good morning, mother," Polly said. "Good morning, father."

Mother and father were up early this morning, or at least earlier than usual. Most mornings, Polly was the first one awake, sometimes by quite a while. But not today.

"Mm," said both her parents without looking up.

Polly took her usual seat at the potato skin table, pulling up a carved potato skin chair to the left of her father, opposite of mother.

"Did you guys sleep okay?" Polly asked, to which she received another distracted, grumbling reply. Both her parents had their heads down, concentrating.

Without looking up, Polly's father reached out for the potato skin pitcher and poured his daughter a glass of potato juice.

"Thank you, father."

"Welcome, Polly."

Polly took a sip of the room temperature juice. Then she picked up her potato skin fork (three prongs, crafted herself) and began to eat in silence. The lack of table conversation was normal on most days. And today was no different. Sometimes families had things to talk about, and the conversation was lively and fun. Most times this was not the case.

Today's breakfast was just-above-room-temperature scrambled yams, as much as you could eat.

Both her parents were busy reading.

"New magazines in the mail last night?" Polly asked as she nibbled the corners of her piled-high plate of scrambled yams. You could, if you chose, eat your plate, since everything inside Yam Hill was edible. Everything from the walls of your room, to eating utensils, even the furniture could all be eaten. Tough, but edible.

Polly tried again. "I said, did you guys receive new magazines in the mail last night?"

"Eat your breakfast, please, Polly," father told her.

She did, quietly.

The rest of breakfast, what little she ate, was swallowed in silence. Both her parents were too involved in their magazines, reading by the dim red LED light of their potato skin lamps.

"Can I go explore with Bic today?" Polly asked.

"Shhh," mother hissed at her. "Eat—your—breakfast—please."

"I did already," Polly said, getting irritated. Her parents got like this every time new magazines or an Elder-approved book came in the mail. Polly could read just fine—very well, actually. But she was one of those rare kids of the potato who actually enjoyed running through the winding hallways and roaming the many unused rooms of Yam Hill.

"Be home by suppertime, please," father said, then readjusted his lamp to read some blurry, or stained, or illegible part of his magazine story. This meant she could have lunch at Bic's house, or anywhere else in the entirety of Yam Hill, depending on how far they explored.

Unlike Old Earth, the people of Yam Hill were always hospitable. Children could rattle the front curtain of a complete stranger (there were always a few, since not everybody on opposite sides of Yam Hill knew each other well) and be invited inside, fed and chatted up for a while, then be sent on their way. Things had been like this for many years, since the creation of Yam Hill.

Polly's best friend inside Yam Hill was a boy her age. His full name was Bic Lighter, pulled from the pages of an Old Earth magazine, twelve, thirteen, maybe even fifteen or sixteen years ago. Although his name had been approved by the Three Elders at the time, that particular name probably would not be allowed today. It was only after the baby was named that it was brought to the Elders' attention that a "lighter" was an Old Earth tool used for starting a fire.

Much like the Old Earth, a large-scale fire would be devastating to the people of the potato. An event such as this could end their way of life.

"Bye, mom! Bye, dad!" Polly was already off and running.

3

Everyone inside Yam Hill considered themselves a survivor. Though not a single current resident of the potato had actually survived anything.

The current generation of Yam Hill, same as the generation before them, and before them, had not actually survived anything either. No one currently living had any recollection of what happened the day the world stopped working properly, bringing an end to all human life.

Except for a small group from Idaho.

They were Stayers, not Survivors. They stayed inside the potato, day after day, year after year. The survival part was their daily lives.

Dark. Hopeless. Tasteless.

4

Clothing for the people of Yam Hill was a non-issue. Unlike Old Earth, where people made a great fuss over clothes, and jewelry, and makeup, it was the complete opposite for potato residents.

Judging by all the faded pictures from Old Earth magazines, all those billions of people who perished during the Great Unexpected Tragedy were incredibly obsessed with all aspects of the human body. This included adorning their bodies with precious metals, such as gold and silver. Two things that no one inside Yam Hill had ever seen, touched, or fully understood.

Some of the magazines that were circulated throughout the potato, year after year, were simply old sales catalogs. These old booklets were loaded with all sorts of strange items that, at one point in human history, were quite common. But these catalogs were also filled with page after page of babies, young children, middle-aged men and women, and even much older people displaying their bodies and showing off their clothing.

Inside Yam Hill, no one cared what you were wearing. So long as you were covered from your neck to your knees, you were free to do as you liked. No one was judged by their clothing, unlike the people of Old Earth, who were appraised by their appearance all those many, many years ago.

All residents of Yam Hill wore the same style of potato attire, made of dried potato skin. Men and women carried out their lives wearing a comfortably loose body covering. Each potato skin covering was pulled over the head, through the large cutout, then wrapped around the body and secured with a long thin strip of potato skin, tied around the waist.

If you were motivated enough, you could make your own body covering. There wasn't much variety in terms of material (fabric), but you could still cut, slice, or even julienne your length of toughened potato skin, then borrow a hole-punch tool from one of the Tool Keepers, plus some thin fiber rope (the equivalent of thread, though nowhere near as fine) and stitch together a new creation.

Clothes Makers were quite common all throughout Yam Hill. But they were not the ones who actually acquired the raw material. It was the Diggers who routinely brought them the 5-foot-by-5-foot sections of uncontaminated potato skin.

Some Digging Crews were focused on expansion, while others carved out potato skins to be used for all things crafted inside the orange walls of Yam Hill.

Carved from the outer edges of their mountain-sized potato habitat, these roughly twenty-five square foot sections of potato skin were cut and peeled, then distributed to the various Clothes Maker's shops, to be worked into wearables. And useable items. Even non-useable items.

Potato skin was never in short supply.

Until recently, there had been a total of thirty-seven Clothes Maker's shops throughout all of Yam Hill. That number had dropped to thirty-five, following the death of not one, but two lifelong Clothes Makers.

Hardly six months had passed since both Mr. and Mrs. Geyser were ceremoniously Ejected from Yam Hill.

Both Mr. and Mrs. Geyser died peacefully in their sleep, though not on the same day. Mr. and Mrs. Geyser, a lovely couple who had been married a long time but chose to work in separate shops, died within one week of each other.

These two quick deaths caused a bit of a scare throughout the potato. Most people simply came to accept the fact that both Mr. Geyser and Mrs. Geyser, whose passing came suddenly and with no preceding illness, had lived a good life, living to the approximate age of 37 and 34, respectively.

Mr. and Mrs. Geyser were each given the highest honors for their Ejection. This included some thoughtful words spoken by some of their closest friends and loyal customers, plus a three-part speech delivered by the Elders.

Afterwards, Mr. and Mrs. Geyser's potato skin wrapped bodies were tossed out of the only exit: a large square cutout at the top of a long, 2,080 step staircase.

Sadly, there was no one to take over either of their long-running shops. Typically, when a Clothes Maker dies—or a Digger, or a Food Group Member, or a Light Checker—the child will take over those duties, carrying on the tradition until their own eventual death.

In the case of Mr. and Mrs. Geyser, there were no children. Even after years of trying to have a child naturally, and even seeking to adopt a child through the rules and regulations of Yam Hill, they had remained childless.

The Three Elders had seen to that.

"...after careful consideration, the other Elders and I have denied your request for a child through the reception process. Because your work is far too important, your request is hereby rejected..."

This verdict caused the young married couple to retreat to their dim, three-room living space, sitting silently in separate rooms for days, not reading, hardly eating.

Eventually, sometime in the middle of the fourth week of grieving, Mr. and Mrs. Geyser pulled through and were able to go on with their potato lives. After coming to terms with the fact that their family would remain only two members, both Mr. and Mrs. Geyser devoted the rest of their lives to making comfortable potato skin coverings for everyone, right up until their final day.

For a resident of Yam Hill, this was considered a fulfilled life.

5

The only job that is not available to the general public is that of becoming an Elder. No one can apply for this all-important job. These jobs were always handed down from an Elder to their eldest son, provided the eldest son showed that he could take on the responsibility of keeping the people of Yam Hill alive for another generation.

This is how the original members of Yam Hill ran things. It was still how things were run today.

The current Three Elders each had at least one son, so an heir for each of them was secure. The current Second Elder has five sons, with another child on the way. One of them will take over for him on the day of his death, ceremonial potato skin wrapping of his body, and final Ejection from Yam Hill. ˜

Throughout the entire recorded history of Yam Hill, there has never been a female Elder. Elders have always been men. There are many women who serve in leadership roles, just not that of Elder.

Three of the Five Food Groups have leaders that are women. The majority of successful shops in Yam Hill are run by women. Many Light Checkers are women, who work hard every day to make sure the hallways and stairwells (at least the commonly used ones) have enough light for safe travel throughout the potato.

Any potato resident can become lost quite easily if they are not careful. One wrong turn is all it takes to set yourself on a panic-filled journey through the labyrinth of Yam Hill, racing upwards, downwards, running up and down a crisscross pattern of seemingly endless hallways and stairwells.

If a resident is unfamiliar with an area and becomes lost, the wise choice is stay where they are until someone comes along to guide them back home. This could take several hours, or several days, depending on where you are in Yam Hill. Typically, no longer than a week if a Search Request was sent (and most importantly, approved) by one of the Elders.

Any resident, young or old, could become disoriented very quickly. Most hallways and stairways look almost exactly alike. Even when you think you have arrived home, you may not be. When this happens, you apologize to your neighbor for bursting in on them, perhaps share a laugh (depending on what was happening when you walked in), then take some directions and make your way back to your own area.

If you do become lost, shouting for help does no good. No one who is not within close proximity can hear you screaming for help. Sound does not travel well through thick walls of yam.

Some residents become lost on purpose.

Their hope is to not be found.

6

Most residents have heard the stories about the Solitaires. The small percentage of residents who live in some of the darkest, purposely under-lit rooms and hallways on the upper levels.

At least once a year, usually after drinking what was supposed to be a life-ending amount of their distilled potato juice, someone from the Solitary area of Yam Hill (male or female) will wander off, never to be seen again. These sad residents often spend their last few hours digging their own grave, which they then crawl into and seal themselves in.

Others are discovered by accident, weeks or months later. If the body is not discovered (and dishonorably Ejected) within roughly a six-to-eight-week time frame, chances are that the body has decomposed enough that it has been absorbed into Yam Hill itself—a rebirth, of sorts. These poor residents, the saddest and most neglected of all people inside Yam Hill, these stewards of loneliness, are set free by way of composting.

7

In the days of Old Earth, people worshiped something called money. Small paper rectangles, varying in colors.

Money has no value inside Yam Hill.

Potato chips are the new currency.

8

Polly was slightly out of breath by the time she rattled her best friend's front curtain. In the days of Old Earth, "knocking" was something most people knew how to do. Inside Yam Hill, balling one's fist and bashing it on a large rectangular section of wood was an ancient formality.

Wood was something no one inside Yam Hill had ever seen, touched, or fully understood. Inside the potato, all residents and families have a front curtain. Long strips of decorative potato skin that you can rattle and draw the attention of the person you seek, provided they are home.

Bic came outside, mostly smiling. His was a nice smile, as was Polly's. Most of their teeth had grown in straight, unlike a lot of residents of Yam Hill. However straight their smiles might be, Bic and Polly's teeth were still tinted orange just like everyone else's.

"Hi, Polly."

"Hi, Bic." Right away she noticed he wasn't his usual moderately happy self. "You okay? What's wrong with you today? You aren't sick, are you?"

Instinctively, Polly took a nervous step backwards. She was worried about being coughed on, or sneezed on, or that she might catch his sickness through some undiscovered means.

When somebody gets sick inside Yam Hill, people become nervous, even paranoid. Sometimes, if sick enough, the ailing one(s) are quarantined in one of the many Sick Rooms on the top floors. It was a common but unspoken fact that these Sick Rooms were purposely built close to the Ejection Site. If the sick person's health was not restored in a reasonable amount of time (reasonable according to the Three Elders, who make all the big decisions), their removal from Yam Hill would be swift.

Sickness, even in its simplest forms, such as a head cold, can lead to not only the death of the one who is ill, but many others.

Basically everyone.

Immune systems are nothing like they were many years ago, when things like vitamins and a balanced diet were quite common—if not utilized, then at least available. A diet of nothing but potatoes will sustain life, not much more.

Bic shook his head. "No, Polly, I'm not sick. Nothing like that. It's just..." His chin sunk to his chest and he didn't talk for a while.

"What is it then?" Polly asked.

"It's my parents," Bic said. "They got their new magazines delivered last night. Lots of people in our area did. My parents hardly said two words to me at breakfast this morning."

Polly folded her arms across her chest.

"Usually we have stuff to talk about," Bic went on. "Or they help me with my recipes. But then their magazines show up…" He practically spat the words out. "Heads down, staring at their magazines like it's the only thing they've got to live for."

Polly buried her own emotions. "That's terrible," she said, though she also felt ignored by her parents.

"They both know I want to be in a Food Group when I'm good enough," Bic said, clearly upset. "And I've been practicing, too, experimenting with different recipes. I've been writing down all my ideas on that potato skin notepad I got for my last birthday. Which reminds me…"

"What?" Polly asked.

Bic scratched his tangled mop of orangish brown hair, which was long, but nowhere near as long as Polly's.

"My potato pen is almost out of ink," Bic said. "Maybe I should just stay home today and make some more."

Knowing him as well as she did, Polly knew that a distraction—something fun—was needed to bring him out of his moderate despair. Otherwise he would talk himself into a depression, then turn around and go back inside after telling her how he can't come out today. Then he'll sit in his room all day, doing nothing, making himself sick, and then she wouldn't see him for a week, or longer.

"Forget about your parents for now, will you?" Polly waved a hand in the direction of Bic's parents, who were both sitting hardly twenty feet away, and probably able to hear her remarks, if only they weren't so engrossed with their magazines. The moment she left her own potato home, she'd quickly forgotten about her own parent troubles, and how much they ignored her.

Bic shrugged and said, "I'll try to happy myself. But— oh, I don't know."

"Come on," Polly said. "I've got something that will happy you right up."

He smiled his crooked little smile. "Where are we going today, Polly? You're not going to get me in trouble again, are you? The last time you told me you had something to show me, we ended up being gone for almost two days. We had to spend the night in Ms. Doppelhammer's room, remember?"

"Ms. Doppelganger," Polly said, correcting him. She took great offense when her best friend either unintentionally or intentionally mispronounced Ms. Doppelganger's name. Polly thought the potato world of Ms. Doppelganger, the incredibly hospitable older woman who lives in the tiny two-room apartment on the opposite side of Yam Hill.

At somewhere in her early forties, Ms. Doppelganger was one of the oldest residents currently living inside the potato. She was well-known on the far side of Yam Hill, though not so much where Polly and Bic's families lived, over two miles away. Polly's wish for when she got that old—that is, if she lived that long—was that she would still be as nice and sweet-mannered (and attractive) as Ms. Doppelganger.

"No, she lives too far away," Bic said. "How about I go see my friends in Food Group Four today. And you can go and visit Ms. Doppelganger. Although..."

Bic momentarily tuned out of the conversation, as he sometimes did.

"Although what, Bic?" Polly had to stand there and wait for him to sort out his thoughts.

Bic was still thinking, apparently very hard. Polly thought they were wasting valuable exploring time.

Finally, Bic spoke his mind: "I wonder why Ms. Doppelganger has so much light in her room? She has ten times the wire, and metal clips, and copper and zinc that most people have. Everybody knows that only the Five Food Groups need that much electricity."

"I don't know, Bic," said Polly. "And I don't care."

As if on cue, speaking about electricity, one of the LED lights that lit the hallway they were standing in suddenly flickered and went out. They would have to inform one of the Light Checkers about this whenever they passed one in the hallway.

As often as Bic travelled to one of the Five Food Groups, trying to get in good with them, that was probably the exact same number of trips Polly had made to Ms. Doppelganger's. Polly would usually stick around for five or ten minutes, become genuinely bored, then head over to Ms. Doppelganger's home.

Ms. Doppelganger had so many wonderful stories to tell about Old Earth, with its blues and greens, fancy yellows and bright reds. Listening to her tell stories made it all seem more real, more fantastic. Much better than just reading the words for herself, straining her eyes to read in the dim single LED light that each occupant of Yam Hill was allowed to have in their private room.

When Polly would come back from her visit, hours later and with a stomach crammed full of Ms. Doppelganger's wonderful potato chips (plus an extra portion to share with Bic), they would walk home together, exchanging stories. The last thing Polly cared about was standing around all day and talking food recipes, or lack thereof.

"Honestly, I don't even know how you make it to her room," Bic said. "I'd get lost in ten minutes."

Polly used to get lost, with so many twists and turns and hallways and stairwells, but not so much anymore. Only rarely did she have to rattle anyone's front curtain to ask for directions, or inquire if she was still headed the right way towards the home of sweet old Ms. Doppelganger.

"Actually, I think I'll just stay home today," Bic said, inching his way back inside. "Maybe tomorrow we can do something together, okay?"

Polly pretended not to hear him. She spun on the heels of her potato skin sandals, then took off running down the dim hallway.

"Polly!" Bic called out. "Where are you going?"

"Come with me!" Polly shouted as she rounded a corner. She was already headed up the potato stairwell.

Despite his conscience telling him to stay home, Bic followed her, as always. They'd been best friends for a long time, so he knew she meant well. She never intended to get him in trouble. It usually just worked out that way. If she wasn't always the most level-headed person, at least she was unpredictable.

Yam Hill was severely lacking in unpredictability.

That's what Bic liked about Polly. That's also why he usually gave in and followed along during these little adventures. There was no way of knowing that this adventure, the one he was reluctantly about to join, would not turn out nearly as well as all the others.

This adventure would end with a double Ejection.

The Three Elders would declare it as: "...the riddance of two harmful and untrustworthy potato residents, Polly Want A Cracker and Bic Lighter, who are hereby forcefully Ejected from Yam Hill..."

While climbing up the potato steps two at a time, then hurrying down the glowing red hallway to catch up to his best friend, Bic felt that rare thrill. The thrill of the unknown. Neither Bic or Polly had any idea that before the day was over, they would both see the outside world.

Old Earth.

It would be the last thing they ever saw.

"Polly, wait up!" Bic hollered. "Ms. Doppelganger's place is the other way!"

From way down at the end of the hallway, Polly shouted: "We're not going to visit Ms. Doppelganger today! We're going to Jack of Hearts!"

Bic lowered his head. Quietly, he said, "Oh no." But his legs kept walking at the same speed. "Not him again. That guy scares me."

Polly shouted at him, again, to hurry up.

Bic did as his best friend asked (*yelled* at him) and hurried to catch up. There was no chance of going back home now.

9

All things in Yam Hill were made of hardened potato skin, including shoes. Close in appearance to Old Earth "sandals," these tough potato skins were wrapped once around the foot, tied together with thin potato skin rope, with both the toes and heel protruding from either end.

Potato foot coverings could be made quite easily, or as often as needed. Such as when children continuously outgrow them during early childhood. As an adult, you simply craft a new pair if they crack, or split, or wear out.

Going barefoot was another option. But this made walking more difficult, especially in the less travelled hallways and stairwells, where the yam flooring can be quite soft.

Most residents of Yam Hill chose to stay extremely local for the entirety of their lives. The general population hardly ever travelled past the few hallways in their immediate area. Their only real travel time involved walking to the monthly Community Meetings. Attendance was mandatory, otherwise these too would've been skipped altogether.

Foot coverings could last for many years, depending on how far a person travelled during their lifetime.

Polly's friend from the other side of Yam Hill, the lovely and sweet Ms. Doppelganger, had worn the same pair of hardened potato skin shoes since she was roughly the age Polly was now. Though for long spells of her life, Ms. Doppelganger was not permitted to do much walking, so this might account for her shoes lasting for over thirty years.

People of Old Earth walked an average of 5,000 steps per day.

People of Yam Hill walk less than 500 steps per day.

10

There are still a few Jewelry Makers inside Yam Hill, though hardly anyone adorned their bodies with those types of things—items such as earrings and necklaces. But they are still routinely created by a few of the most talented and nimble fingers. These handcrafted items were viewed as some of the most beautiful creations inside the potato.

Currently, there are three Jewelry Makers living in Yam Hill. None of these shops are located in the same area, as there are no designated shopping areas like there were in the days of Old Earth. All three viewing rooms, where these potato treasures could be seen, were next door to each of the Jewelry Makers' private living area.

One of the most well-respected and well-liked Jewelry Makers was a frightfully thin but very pretty woman named Ms. Mulberry. Her full name was Mulberry Wine, same as the hard-to-read sign outside her shop.

<h1 style="text-align:center">Mulberry Wine</h1>
<h2 style="text-align:center">Handcrafted Potato Creations</h2>

Despite being only in her late-twenties, or perhaps early-thirties, she had given up on the idea of ever finding a husband, or having children with whom she could share her carving talent. Her studio had literally hundreds upon hundreds of fascinating potato skin creations. Much more than the other two Jewelry Makers combined, both of which had been doing the same thing for much longer.

Many residents supposed that Ms. Mulberry focused all her time on her work because she was without a family to care for. Mulberry Wine was quite pretty, approachable and available, so perhaps it was her obvious skill that men disliked. Possessing an actual *talent* was not altogether common inside Yam Hill.

There was also old Mr. Mercantile, a widower who lost his wife more than a decade ago, and who now passed his lonely days whittling away on hardened chunks of potato. From his waking moment until he laid his head back down on his potato bed with his soft, mashed yam pillow, Mr. Mercantile could always be found inside his shop, meticulously folding and creasing, cutting and shaping, bending and manipulating a piece of potato skin into some new beautiful orange and brown creation that no one would ever bargain for, but would certainly offer the most wonderful compliments.

To him, it didn't matter if nobody wanted to barter for any of his creations. He would've gladly exchanged any one of them for a handful of potato chips or even a container of fresh potato juice. To lonely old Mr. Mercantile, he swore he could feel his wife's presence while he made his wonderful creations in his tiny studio. And he knew that one day, when his own Ejection had come due, he would once again be reunited with his wife.

And lastly, there was Charity Filibuster, a married woman with three children of her own. Two children were from her current husband, whom she separated from two potato years ago, but had since gotten back together with. Although the relationship she had was brief (with a Solitaire man, who had recently self-Ejected), the surprise relationship produced a little boy.

Now reunited with her husband, once again living under the same potato roof, she is now teaching all three of her children the crafting techniques she'd learned from her wonderful teacher, Mr. Mercantile. He was the one who had originally gotten her started in potato skin crafting when she was sixteen, or fifteen, but no older than seventeen years old, just prior to having her first potato child.

Most men and women, and certainly all the curious children, would stop by a Jewelry Maker's shop if they were in the area, to see what new creations were stacked on the potato shelves.

Although a trip like this happened only once, maybe twice, but certainly no more than three times in any given potato year, the visits were long and thoughtful. Sometimes these visits lasted for hours, while the proud Jewelry Maker described the painstaking process of potato skin crafting. Although hardly anything ever left their store shelves, it was nice to know that all the Jewelry Makers' hard work was enjoyed and appreciated.

II

Makeup was something else that the people of Yam Hill did not care for. Although this particular concept was well understood—painting one's face up to appear more attractive—it was not common practice anymore.

People looked how they looked. Usually wild-haired and thin, with a radiant glow to their orange skin. Nobody cared how you presented yourself, only that you were alive and reasonably healthy.

Women of Old Earth, at least most women, but some men too, would paint their faces up to present themselves for public display, or to look more beautiful, or simply because it was accepted (or even expected) by their culture.

Women of Yam Hill, who made up roughly 35% of the population, were nurturing and makeup-free. They did not use Old Earth items such as razors. They did not ornate themselves with jewelry. And they certainly did not spend time worrying about things like hairstyles.

Life was hard for everyone. And looking beautiful for each other was deemed a pointless (or even ridiculous) idea, created by the people of Old Earth.

Rumors still persisted of the early days of Yam Hill, where great parties were thrown. Makeup and costumes were said to be worn. And yet when asked, the Three Elders always denied these old stories with a smile and a good chuckle, telling residents to: "…leave the past in the past, and look forward to the future…" or any number of positive and thoughtful words of encouragement.

Nowadays, the only time a party is thrown is when a young man or woman (or even an older resident) is assigned to a new position, such as being elected to a Food Group, or a Light Checker, or Digger. Even then these parties were very small, usually involving only close family or friends, or perhaps a few neighbors who want to stop by and wish the recipient well.

Events like Christmas, or New Year's Day, or July 4th could not be pinpointed, so were not celebrated anymore. Those events died along with everything else during the Great Unexpected Tragedy. Even if you decided (for some reason) to celebrate one of these ancient, Old Earth anniversaries, it had to be done inside your own potato home, involving as few people as possible.

The current Three Elders were making a small push to invent a yearly, or possibly a biannual tradition specifically for the ongoing survival of the people of the potato. This would not be in lieu of the monthly meetings, which were merely a way of keeping all residents in touch with what was currently happing inside the protected walls of Yam Hill.

This new celebration would be created to suit all residents, young and old. All those who were brave enough to keep enduring day to day. For those who wanted to enrich their potato lives with as much vitamin A and beta-carotene as they possibly could.

The Three Elders were mainly having trouble deciding how long the festivity should be. None of them wanted it to drag on for days, or even more than a few hours. At the last Elder's meeting, they'd decided that the celebration should last for at least one full evening. The final decision could end up taking years to settle, so there was no hurry. Until then, people of the potato would have to find their own happiness and their own reasons to celebrate.

Laughter is scarce in Yam Hill. So are reasons to celebrate. And even though thick potato walls deadened sound extremely well, people still liked things to remain quiet in all areas of Yam Hill.

Sometimes even screaming went unheard.

12

Hobbies are in short supply inside Yam Hill. That is why Old Earth books and magazines are so popular. They provide an escape from the daily yam.

13

Every day is the same.
Every meal is the same.

14

Polly rattled the front curtain again.

"I wonder where he is?" Polly asked. "Why isn't he answering? Last time I saw Jack of Hearts, he told me to come and visit him in four or five days. I think it's been that long...maybe." Polly tried to remember exactly how many days had passed since she'd last spoken to Jack of Hearts, her most trusted adult friend, besides Ms. Doppelganger.

Bic groaned. "We came all the way up here," he said, cautiously joining her by the front curtain, "and you don't even know if he's home or not?"

"Did you just say 'all the way up here,' Bic?" Polly gave him a look. "You've barely gone up two flights of stairs, down three hallways, and here we are. Stop complaining. You'd never go anywhere if it wasn't for me. Just like most people around here, you never want to leave home."

Bic could hold his own when being insulted by his best friend. "Those staircases are longer than most the other ones in our area," he said. "And it's practically four hallways to get here, not three."

Polly wasn't in the habit of rolling her eyes. It was more of a blink, look one way, blink again, then look the other way.

"Bic? If it wasn't for me practically dragging you out of your room this morning," Polly said, "you'd be at home right now, completely bored."

To Bic, being at home right now sounded like a much better idea.

"Polly, I don't even know why I came up here with you," Bic said. "Jack of Hearts doesn't approve of me. I don't know why, but I'm certain he dislikes me."

Bic never understood why, but Jack of Hearts had always made him uneasy. Not just because of his size, being one of the largest men in all of Yam Hill, but possibly it was because Jack of Hearts worked for the Three Elders, the most powerful men in Yam Hill.

Polly gave him a little shove. "Jack of Hearts approves of you just fine, Bic. He just—" Polly tried to quickly think of something to say, but Bic was right. Jack of Hearts always did seem a little bit nervous around Bic.

For years, ever since they were kids, it had always been that way. It was as if Jack of Hearts was worried that Bic might tell someone about what he and Polly had talked about, or report the conversation to someone. Most times during a visit, Bic would sit on one of the extra-long potato couches and eat his way through Jack of Hearts' massive supply of potato chips.

"I can't help it if he trusts me more than he trusts you," Polly finally said. "Jack of Hearts is the nicest person I know. Except for maybe Ms. Doppelganger. He's been babysitting me since I was a..."

"A baby?" Bic suggested. "Yes, I know. You've only told me about seventeen million times. But what I want to know is..." He tuned out again.

"What?" Polly asked.

Bic looked confused. "I was just wondering why your friend always has so many potato chips," he asked. "They're hard to get for normal people—people like us. But he always has a lot of them. More than I've ever seen."

"Jack of Hearts is a Digger," Polly reminded him. "Diggers all get a ration of potato chips for all their hard work."

"I know that, Polly," Bic said, giving her a critical look. "But he always has more potato chips than anybody I know. Potato chips are handed out only by the Three Elders, and only on very special occasions. But every time we come up here, Jack of Hearts has almost an entire room filled with potato chips. Huge potato skin bags of them."

Polly had never once given this any thought. Jack of Hearts was a Digger, and Diggers all receive one ration of potato chips per seven work days. She assumed that he saved them up for when he had visitors.

"Yes," Polly said, nodding her head. "You do enjoy eating his potato chips, don't you? So don't complain so much when I bring you up here for a visit."

"Fine," Bic said, dropping his chin.

Polly rattled the front curtain a fifth time.

"If he is at work, maybe he won't mind if we go inside for a minute and, you know..." Bic's voice trailed off. He looked embarrassed as he stood there in the dim light of the hallway. He was hoping maybe they could go inside and help themselves to a handful (or two) of potato chips.

"We are not going into his room uninvited," Polly told him, with her hands on her hips. "Not so you can take home a bunch of his potato chips. You can forget that idea."

Not once in her potato existence had Polly ever entered Jack of Hearts' room uninvited. Or any room, for that matter. Yam Hill residents may live a moderately dark life inside a potato, but they were still aware of proper human etiquette.

Bic understood. "Okay. Fine. So now what?"

"Well, if he's not here," Polly said. "I guess we can come back later to—"

"PSSSSSST!"

Both Polly and Bic jumped several feet. They'd never heard anything like this. Such a strange sound. Both of them, their hearts, were absolutely racing by this point, thumping underneath their potato skin coverings.

"Polly? What was that?" Bic was looking up and down the hallway, one way then the other.

Polly was doing the same thing.

The noise sounded angry noise, not even human. Perhaps one of the animals they'd read about in some Old Earth book or magazine—snakes and elephants—somehow made its way into Yam Hill.

"That's impossible," Polly thought. She knew as well as anyone else that absolutely everything—lakes, oceans, all people, all animals—all disappeared off the face of Old Earth during the Great Unexpected Tragedy.

In all their years, neither of them had been hissed at like this. People in Yam Hill didn't make such noises at each other. Residents spoke to each other with civility, in calm and soft-spoken voices.

"Psssst!" came the strange noise again.

Bic was ready to bolt. So was Polly, but she managed to steady her feet.

Then a human voice asked: "Polly, is that you?"

Looking up and down the dim hallway, then finally looking up, Polly spotted the noisemaker. It was a human making that noise, after all. Not some ancient monster from Old Earth.

"Jack of Hearts, is that you? What are you doing way up there?" Polly had to stretch her neck and stand on her tiptoes to even catch a glimpse. The hallway was too dark to see clearly, so she wasn't entirely sure it was him.

"Yes, it's me," said Jack of Hearts in a hushed voice. "Up and to your left."

Polly saw half his face and relaxed. She waved, thinking this must be some kind of practical joke, him being up near the ceiling. But Jack of Hearts couldn't wave back. He didn't have room to wave, or even turn over. He only had enough room to hide, to lie still, up where no one would find him.

"What are you doing up there?" Polly asked. "I guess an even better question is how did you get up there?"

Instead of answering, it was more questions.

"Who's that with you?" asked Jack of Hearts, trying to squeeze his head out of a very small opening to get a glimpse of the second person. Bic was trying to stay out of sight, so he wasn't helping much. Hearing voices from high above your head was certainly not typical inside Yam Hill. It scared him so badly that he put his back against the nearest potato wall, and remained there.

"Is that you, Bic?" asked Jack of Hearts. "Answer me, dammit. Right now!"

"Yes, it's me," Bic said, refusing to come into view. He stood stiff against the wall.

"Get over here," Polly said, grabbing Bic's arm and forcing him to stand beside her. She wanted to show him that it was only them, no one else.

"Just you two?" asked Jack of Hearts, which Polly thought was an odd question.

"Answer me!" Jack hissed.

Polly flinched. Having never been spoken to in this manner before, not ever, she didn't know how to respond. It was always just the two of them. Once in a great long while, Polly's mother or father would come up for a quick visit, but other than those rare occasions, it was only Polly and Bic that ever came to visit, or just Polly herself.

"Yes, Jack, it's just the two of us," Polly answered, all the while wondering what was wrong with him. Why was he so angry? What was so different about today?

The hallway was silent for a long time.

"Come inside," Jack of Hearts said, then rolled out of sight. He reappeared a moment later at the main entrance. "Quickly. Before anyone sees you."

Polly was waving at Bic, urging him to hurry up and get inside.

Bic mouthed the words "before anyone sees us?" as he walked passed Polly, on his way inside the room. He was shaking his head. He had never in his whole life wanted to go home as badly as he did right now.

Polly was nervous, too. But Jack of Hearts was her friend. And if he was in some kind of trouble, she wanted to help.

15

There are many jobs inside Yam Hill. Employment is not a requirement for adult residents, but it was always encouraged by the Three Elders.

Most residents preferred a life of leisure.

16

Married couples are absolutely permitted inside Yam Hill. These pairings are often arranged by the Elders, but not always. Two people who had simply enjoyed each other's company over the years could come to a mutual agreement: To live together, in relative harmony, in the same potato home, be kind and courteous to one another, and attempt to have children.

"Naturally, if possible," one of the Three Elders would state during the marriage ceremony. "Otherwise through the Reception process."

Inside Yam Hill, reception is the equivalent of adoption, which was popular during the days of Old Earth. Through either means, by conception or reception, a child always brings joy to a new family.

Children can also introduce many new challenges for even the happiest and most committed potato couple. Bringing up a child inside Yam Hill is no easy task.

Until they reach the age where they can go off on their own and explore, children are usually kept inside. They are brought up and trained to the best of their parent's ability. Help is always available from other members of the potato community. Especially if the parents cannot read particularly well, or know little about the history of the potato, or about the laws of Yam Hill.

The Three Elders would make random visits (inspections) to make sure the child was being fed properly, and being adequately nurtured. The Three Elders would often interview neighbors of the new parents to make sure the child's needs were being met.

If misinformed, or flat out lied to about the welfare of a child, even something like not routinely changing the child's potato skin diaper, the Elders would not only punish the parents, but also the neighbors who failed to inform them about any injustice done to a child. This is literally never the case, as every resident of Yam Hill understands how precious life is, even if that life is spent inside an overgrown potato.

"Children are a precious gift," the First Elder was fond of saying. "I myself have not only children living inside this great yam of ours, but also grandchildren."

Hurting a child, either physically or mentally, or endangering a child in any way, those were all things that belonged to Old Earth. The only way a child might get hurt inside Yam Hill is if they had a misstep climbing up a potato stairwell and went tumbling down, or if they were jumping off some potato furniture and crash-landed. But even then, a child getting hurt was rare, since the entire inside of Yam Hill was quite soft.

All children of Yam Hill were safe and well fed.

This was quite unlike the days of Old Earth, where it was not only possible to starve to death, but actually happened throughout the world on a daily basis.

Running out of food in Yam Hill was not a concern. Not for anyone. And especially not a concern for young children, who were prone to reaching out and grabbing a scoop or handful of their neighbor's front wall, or even ripping down a section of someone else's front curtain and chewing on that. Although all parts of the Yam Hill community were edible, residents generally preferred that you did not eat the walls surrounding their potato home.

17

The idea of a school inside Yam Hill had been tried throughout the years, then usually discontinued due to poor attendance.

The question would always arise: Why would anyone wake up early, walk a great distance to someone else's room, sit quietly while someone else tries to teach you things you may already know, and then be forced to walk all the way home when the teaching session was over?

Most kids preferred to stay at home. They could pick up on the few things their parents had learned through the years, then go off on their own, reading the same Elder-approved books and magazines that their parents read, and learn at their own pace.

Another reason to not open any kind of formal education program was the simple fact that there might not be enough children alive at the time to make it worthwhile.

Inside the protective covering of Yam Hill, sometimes only a small handful of children exist at any one time. Oftentimes, they all live on opposite sides of the potato, or scattered throughout. This can make travel times very long. Children having time to interact with other children becomes challenging. And any sort of challenge, or introducing any kind of difficulty into a parent's life is something that most residents of Yam Hill are not accustomed to, and would rather avoid.

Polly and Bic were approximately the same age, born within a few months of each other. After the two of them arrived in Yam Hill, not a single child was born for more than three years. Bic was feared to be the last child.

According to the old record books, which the Elders say go back hundreds and hundreds of years, this was the longest "child drought" in the history of Yam Hill.

After that long and stressful time without a single new potato child, several happy couples reported that they were expecting. Once again, the birth rate was back up where it should be, with anywhere from one to five, or sometimes as many as seven or eight children born per year.

Still, the fear of the lastborn potato child was always in the back of everyone's mind. That is why married couples (and otherwise) try their best to prolong potato life.

18

What food the human body cannot process must, itself, be Ejected. It is a fact of human existence. The creators of Yam Hill, the original members, took steps in the early days to ensure that all inhabitants could rid their bodies of waste products in the privacy of their own home. What was once called a "bathroom" during the days of Old Earth was now referred to as a waste room.

Some people's living quarters had multiple waste rooms. That depended on how large the family was, or how far (or how little) you wanted to travel when your body informed you that it was time. It was up to each individual potato family (or single person) to decide how badly they wanted a second, third, or fourth waste room in their home. If you wanted to add another waste room—or sleep room, or storage room, or any other kind of room—you simply carved it out of the walls.

Outwards, preferably, not up or down.

There were many stories about some eager couple digging in the wrong direction, and ended up closer than ever to their next-door neighbor. These persistent rumors, though they could never be pinpointed, always made the rounds whenever someone was remodeling their potato home.

It was common knowledge that back during the early days of Yam Hill, several people (the number having grown over the years, ranging anywhere from two people, all the way up to 250 people, or more) were killed while carving out the main tunnels and hallways that were still used today. The Three Elders never seemed to confirm or deny these rumors, so most residents thought them true, at least to some degree.

Public waste rooms (built far away from any food supply) were located all throughout Yam Hill, so there was never any reason to worry.

Over the course of many decades, Diggers worked very hard to carve out these relief stations. These large hollow wells were all ten, twenty, sometimes thirty feet deep, or more. When full, they were merely sealed up with thick potato paste, and a new waste room was created.

Waste relief in a public hallway was strictly forbidden.

If you are caught doing so, punishment was inevitable, though not very severe. No one had ever been Ejected for relieving themselves in a public place. The culprit was typically forced to join a Digging crew for a week, or a month, depending on which form of bodily relief had taken place.

And even if the urge came along at the most unexpected time, when the traveler was unsure of where the nearest public waste room was located, a simple rattle of someone's front curtain, usually followed by a brief explanation, and practically any resident of Yam Hill would let you inside to use their waste room.

Even though all 604 residents of Yam Hill weren't the closest of friends, they were all neighbors. They were all in this together, sharing their lives inside the hallways, corridors, and glowing red rooms of Yam Hill.

19

The inside of most people's living area looked almost exactly alike. Carved walls that were mostly vertical, but usually sculpted at an odd angle, with a cutout entrance leading into each room. There was never much to look at, as far as decorations went. Sometimes a few potato skin paintings hung on the wall, or perhaps a few designs may have been carved out (or eaten), or maybe even some extra furniture for guests to sit on when (or if) they ever stop by.

People of Old Earth had great huge homes, comparably—at least, in some cases. In other cases, those ancient homes were not that much different from the residences of Yam Hill. Old Earth homes could be made of wood, brick, mud, clay, or even cloth fabric. None of which were available or even fully understood by potato residents.

Homes were now made of yam, with varying degrees of sameness.

Then there was Jack of Hearts' home.

Jack of Hearts' home was the complete opposite of any normal potato residence. All twelve of his rooms were unlike anything else inside Yam Hill.

What was once a small four-room living area, back when Jack's mother and father were alive, had grown to the length of one entire hallway. Room after room, each leading into the next by way of one, two, sometimes three different entryways, all of varying size. Some you had to get down on your hands and knees and crawl through, which were made specifically for Polly and her best friend, Bic, when they were young and loved to crawl around on the floor and play silly childhood games.

Whereas Polly's home and Bic's home, and every other home across the entirety of Yam Hill, looked almost exactly alike, no two rooms in Jack of Hearts' living area looked even remotely the same. Each proceeding room was as different as Jack could dream up. Some even had secret entrances, or secret hiding spots. His oversized rooms were always being added to, carved out, or extended.

Since Jack of Hearts had no neighbors in his immediate area, he was allowed to dig in any direction—within reason, of course. The expansion must be approved by the Three Elders, of course. But his approvals for excavation were never an issue, since he had worked for them since he was sixteen, or fifteen, or perhaps as young as fourteen years old.

And because no one inside the potato had the imagination or the drive that Jack of Hearts possessed (at least in terms of digging), his extended living area was a wonderland to explore.

Whenever Polly asked him how he dreamed these things up, and how he came to invent all the games and experiments and fun things to do at his place, Jack of Hearts would smile, or stroke her long orange hair, but never tell his secrets.

This was also part of the reason that, year after year, Polly would visit him so often. Because Jack of Hearts loved to have fun, which was rare in adults.

At least once or twice a week, sometimes every other day, she would walk up to see him, with or without Bic. Polly would've loved to visit him every single day, but mother and father wouldn't allow it.

"Let Jack of Hearts have a day off from your constant visiting, Polly," father would tell her. "He needs his rest like everyone else. You know he works very hard at his digging job."

And then her mother would usually say something similar. "And his job working for our very respectable Elders."

Jack of Hearts never turned Polly away. Not even when asked to work extra-long hours during a dig, or when he was gone for days at a time working for the Three Elders, or even when he was so exhausted he could hardly keep his eyes open.

More than a few times over the years, Polly had gone up to visit him in the morning, or afternoon, or after dinner—all of which came at different times for everyone—and rattled his front curtain, only to find that he must be at work.

Walking away, she would hear a tired, groggy voice say: "Polly? Please come back."

Jack of Hearts would force himself to stay awake, not wanting to pass up an opportunity to talk with Polly. They would both drink potato juice and eat potato chips, and talk for hours.

Today, things had changed.

There was no time for playing games. No time for eating and drinking. Only one thing was in their near future, and that was a dishonorable Ejection from Yam Hill. All because of their association with a condemned man.

20

Because Jack of Hearts was one of the largest, strongest, most incredibly hard-working, and most loyal people living in Yam Hill, he had been assigned to work for the Three Elders. He was the only employee working for the Elders.

Now they wished him silenced.

The Three Elders had taken a vote. The verdict was unanimous. All three Elders quickly came to the decision that Jack of Hearts needed to be permanently removed from the inner sanctity of Yam Hill, the protective barrier between them and the uninhabitable outside world.

Already once today they had come looking for Jack of Hearts, only to find him missing. But eventually he would return home, and they would come looking for him once again.

In fact, they were already on their way.

21

Jack of Hearts' room was a disaster. Worse than a disaster. It looked like someone (or multiple people) had gone through his entire living quarters, room by room, purposely poking huge holes in the walls, cutting and slashing, and in some cases tearing the walls down completely.

Polly's mind could hardly comprehend it.

Someone was looking for her friend. And that somebody (or somebodies) wanted to find him very badly. And judging by the wild mess, the chaos, and the destroyed potato furniture, they hadn't been able to locate him. Whoever wanted to find Jack of Hearts, they clearly intended to do him harm.

Carved into the potato wall was one word.

Ejected

<h1 style="text-align:center">22</h1>

"Jack, what happened here?" Polly asked the moment she stepped inside—was *pulled* inside, along with Bic. "What happened to your beautiful room?"

All the fun things, including the slide she would shoot down on a square piece of potato skin when she was a child, and the beautifully crafted tossing game that Jack had carved especially for her, and all the paintings she'd made for him when she was little (which he refused to take down), and the furniture, and basically everything...all of it destroyed.

What Polly noticed first was the damage.

What Bic noticed first was the missing hair.

"Forget the room, Polly," Bic said. "What happened to his hair? And where did his beard go?"

Polly had been too shocked at the state of her friend's living area to notice the incredible difference in Jack of Hearts' physical appearance.

All men in Yam Hill, every single one of them—including Polly's father and Bic's father—wore beards and long hair. Getting a hair reduction, what was referred to as a haircut in the days of Old Earth, was extremely painful. That's why most men chose to put it off as long as they could. Usually until the hair on their head or face was so long and bothersome that a trim was necessary.

Jack of Hearts' hair was gone. All the way gone, cut down to short, prickly spikes that jutted out from the top and sides of his skull. Neither Polly or Bic had ever seen hair like this—so short. Only when a baby is born is hair ever this short. They'd seen such a thing in an Old Earth magazine before, a man or woman with a shaved head, but never in real life. Never on an actual resident of Yam Hill.

Even the Three Elders had relatively long, orange-colored hair and a beard. Although theirs were always trimmed quite nicely—the complete opposite of all other male residents. Most people assumed the Three Elders took it upon themselves to get a bi-yearly, possibly even a monthly hair reduction, suffering all the eye-watering pain it took to remove hair from the top of one's head.

Facial hair reductions were more common, but only slightly less painful. And yet, the Three Elders had very thin beards, almost bare skin on their faces. They were praised and respected simply for that.

But no one in Yam Hill had short hair like this.

Not even close.

Jack of Hearts was sitting on the underside of his extra-long chair because it had been flipped over and demolished. His strong hands were rubbing nervously against his short spiky hair. His legs were bouncing up and down as if he could not sit still. And he kept repeating the same words over and over, frightening his two young guests.

"I knew I shouldn't have told him," Jack of Hearts was saying, mostly to himself. He was scratching nervously, and shaking his head. "I knew I couldn't trust him. I knew it. And now look what he did. Look what he did!"

Jack of Hearts might as well be alone, because he had no idea that he had two frightened guests staring at him in the dim red glow of LED lights, all of which had been left untouched by the intruders.

"Jack?" Polly said quietly. When he didn't answer, didn't even hardly realize that she was still in the room with him, she stepped closer.

"Jack? It's me, Polly." She put a hand on his shoulder.

His eyes flashed.

For a moment, Polly thought he was going to lash out at her. His eyes were so fierce, so angry, giving him a deranged sort of appearance.

"I should've killed him," Jack mumbled. But the other two people in the room heard him just fine. "I should've just used my digging shovel to kill him. I should've done it. Right there in the hallway when I had the chance. Soon as everybody turned the corner. I could've buried him in the wall and nobody would've ever found him..."

Now the two young visitors were both alarmed. Even Polly was thinking this was the wrong day, the absolute worst day, to come up here for a visit. Her friend was clearly not himself today. That person was gone. In his place was this quivering, strange-talking, shaved head, mess of a man.

"...should've killed him dead."

Bic was also protective of Polly. In a friendly way, he loved her. And he would not, absolutely *refused*, to allow his best friend to stand that close to a madman.

"Yes. Should've killed him. Should've killed that lying—"

"JACK!" Polly shouted.

That finally got his attention.

"You're scaring me," Polly said, and she meant it. Talking about death is not a comfortable subject, not for any resident of Yam Hill. And death was certainly never spoken about in a threatening way—exactly what Jack of Hearts was doing now.

"Who are you going to kill?" Bic wanted to know. "Why?"

"Yes. Why?" Polly said. "What did this man do?"

Jack of Hearts extended his arms, gesturing for them to look at the full extent of the surrounding destruction.

"This, Polly. He did this." Then he moved so they could see the carved word—EJECTED—on the wall directly behind his head.

"And that," Jack of Hearts said. He pointed to the deadly word as both Polly and Bic leaned in, closer and closer, so they could finally read what was carved into the wall. As soon as they read it, their two heads reared back, eyes wide and fearful. They quickly stepped away from the wall, and away from that word, for the simple reason that it was the very thing that every resident of Yam Hill feared above all.

Jack's chin sank to his chest, but his words were clear: "They're coming for me. I don't know when, but they're coming."

Bic's orange cheeks flushed. "We have to leave, Polly. Right now. I don't care what you say, we have to get out of here. Whatever trouble he's in—" He flicked an accusing finger at Jack of Hearts. "It doesn't include us. Let's leave this place while we still can, okay? Polly, come on!"

Polly refused to leave.

Even when Bic grabbed her arm, she ripped it away from him. Polly stood next to Jack of Hearts, her good friend for all these years, who now desperately needed help. Her heart ached to see him like this, so broken and confused, even scared.

She gently touched the top of his head.

That was all it took to send him over the edge.

Jack of Hearts sobbed, crying his eyes out in front of his two young guests. Bic was appalled. He actually felt ashamed for the big man who was now weeping like a child. Polly felt nothing but love for her grownup friend, and a great desire to fix whatever was wrong.

After a moment, Jack of Hearts finally got his emotions under control. He gently pulled Polly's hand off his shaved head and held it in his own bruised and bloodied hands. She had liked the way it felt, his hair, so fuzzy and prickly to the touch.

"Whatever you believe is wrong, I'm sure we can fix it," Polly said, meaning every word of it. "I promise you, we will find a way to get you out of trouble. Right, Bic?"

Bic flinched. "Yeah. Sure. Exactly as you say. Can we leave now?"

"Thank you, Polly," said Jack of Hearts, wiping at his cheeks. He took a few deep breaths and slowly became the large, strong man she knew him to be. "Thank you for always being so…" He nearly broke down again trying to say the word *kind*.

"So you're willing to let us help you?" asked Polly.

Jack of Hearts shook his head. "You don't understand, Polly. There are so many things that everyone living in Yam Hill don't understand. Especially you, Polly. There were many times I wanted to tell you, to explain to you how this place really works, but I…I just can't."

Jack of Hearts looked beaten, absolutely lost.

"So explain it to me," Polly said. "Or better yet, why don't all three of us go down to see the Three Elders and figure this out. Whatever it is, I'm sure they can help. They oversee everything in Yam Hill, so I'm sure they can—"

"NO!" Jack of Hearts had never looked more serious. He took her by both her hands, drawing her closer. "Promise me, Polly, that you will never go and talk to the Three Elders."

"I..." Polly was so confused that she could hardly speak. Making it even harder to answer was the fact that Jack of Hearts now had her by the upper arms, and was shaking her, demanding that she promise to stay away from the Three Elders.

"Hey! Stop shaking her like that!" Bic shouted, ready to defend his friend. He didn't know exactly what was going on, but he certainly didn't like the way he was holding her, or the fact that he was attempting to force her to make a promise she didn't want to make. Promises, both big and small, were taken very seriously inside Yam Hill. Which was part of the reason Polly didn't answer him right away.

"I promise," Polly finally said. "Whatever it is you say I must promise to, I'll do it."

Bic slapped both hands on top of his head. "Great, Polly. Just great! You just made a promise—to him, of all people—and you don't even know what you promised. Promises are serious, Polly, in case you've forgotten."

Spinning around to face him in the dim light, Polly angrily confronted her best friend. "I haven't forgotten anything, Bic. Now be quiet, or I'm going to..." She trailed off, her anger defusing quickly.

"Or you'll what?" said Bic defiantly, standing there in the red light with both of his bony hands on his bony hips. "Cut all my hair off so I can look like him?" Again, he flicked one hand towards Jack of Hearts, as if he was something disgusting instead of a very large Digger who could easily cause him harm.

"No, I'll probably just punch you so hard you won't be able to breathe properly for the rest of your life," Polly said, meaning every threatening word. "Now be quiet."

Jack of Hearts stood up, a massive mountain of a man. Nobody, not even him, knew exactly what was going on. There was something he needed to show Polly, and it had to be done quickly.

Time was running out.

Time had run out.

"Do you trust me?" asked Jack of Hearts, locking eyes with her. "Polly, do you trust me?"

After stumbling for a moment, unable to speak, Polly nodded that yes, she did trust him. It would've been impossible for her to say no. Not only because of their longtime bond, but also because of the way he looked right now.

"Of course I trust you," Polly said.

"Then promise me," Jack of Hearts said, this time letting her go. "Promise me that if the Three Elders ever come to you and offer you a job..." He stopped to make absolutely certain he had her full attention.

Polly said, "I'm listening. I promise."

"I want you to tell them no," Jack of Hearts told her. "Whatever you do, tell them no, you are not interested. They will try to persuade you and trick you into saying yes. They'll try to tell you that what they're offering you is the most important job inside Yam Hill. It will be done in such a way that it will confuse your thinking. Just like they've done to other pretty girls in the past. They'll probably say the job they are offering you is even more important than their job of being Elders, of governing over all these people."

Polly was trying to follow along. Bic too, but he was still concerned that if he made another move, or said anything else, Polly would ball up her fist and hit him. They'd been friends a long time, and he knew very well how hard she could punch.

"They will lie to you, Polly," explained Jack of Hearts. "That's what they do. They lie. Believe me, if there's anyone inside Yam Hill who knows all of their dirty little secrets…"

Jack of Hearts began to dig through the mess in the food preparation room, what was formerly called a kitchen in the days of Old Earth. He was tossing things out of his way, searching for something specific. Eating utensils, potato skin bowls, decorations, even pieces of smashed furniture were angrily kicked out of the way. Then, surprising even himself, he found exactly what he was looking for among the mess and chaos.

A sharp, hooked item.

Two of them.

Whatever he was holding, they were definitely not manufactured inside Yam Hill. These strange items were from Old Earth.

How they got inside Yam Hill was the question.

23

The original creator of the potato was an extraordinary man called Mr. Yamhill. He single-handedly saved a small group of people from the Great Unexpected Tragedy. And from that small group, the 604 people currently living inside Yam Hill were eventually created.

Everyone knew that Mr. Yamhill was a great, great man. It was not common knowledge, however, that among other important things, he was also a gardener.

24

"What are those?" Bic asked.

Polly was wondering the same thing. "They look like hands."

To simply describe them would take some serious discussion, since neither one of them had seen anything like it. These strange creations were pulled out of a secret compartment that was hidden inside another secret compartment. Jack of Hearts held one in each hand as he dropped to his knees, about to strike.

"Stand back!" ordered Jack of Hearts, and the two of them stood way back. "These are from Old Earth, but they're still sharp." Then he took the strange hooks and jabbed them forcefully into the potato floor and pulled upwards.

"Oof!" Jack grunted, then fell forward. The floor didn't budge.

Polly asked if he was okay.

"Wrong spot," Jack of Hearts said, shrugging his wide shoulders. "It's hard to tell in this great big mess. If I had some proper sunlight…"

They watched as Jack of Hearts searched the area, trying to remember.

Leaning in close, Bic whispered to Polly, "Did he just say sunlight?"

Without receiving an answer, or even a sign that Polly had heard him, Bic pressed harder.

"What is he talking about?" Bic asked, making sure to whisper. "How can a person actually see sunlight? It's only in books."

In a quiet but firm voice, Polly said, "Silence your mouth, Bic. I mean it. I don't want to hear another word from you."

Again, Jack of Hearts jabbed the spiked hands into the potato floor. This time he aimed correctly and up came a large, cubed section of the floor. As it came up, they could see that this large section of potato flooring was tapered at one end, so it would slide right back into place and remain hidden. Polly and Bic had been standing right where Jack of Hearts lifted it from, and neither one of them had noticed it. In the dim red light, the hidden compartment would've been impossible to see.

As he pulled, Jack of Hearts spoke in a strained voice: "You should see the giant light the Three Elders get to enjoy. You'd be amazed. They have a light so bright that it hurts your eyes to look at. Especially when you spend your life in darkness, as we do. But those disgusting liars won't let anyone see it for themselves. They'd rather keep us all in the dark. They're all a bunch of lying hypocrites."

Wisely, Bic kept his mouth shut. But he did not like this rude man making rude comments about the First, Second, and Third Elders, the most loved and respected men in all of Yam Hill. Children were taught that the Elders were respectable, highly regarded, trustworthy men who protected them from the terrible dangers of the outside world.

Jack of Hearts lifted up the section of flooring and tossed it to the side. This would be the last time he would have to uncover it. The secret buried underneath had to be revealed someday. And today was the day.

Buried underneath was a scroll.

This section of potato skin, which Jack of Hearts had been writing in since he was a teenager, was longer than any piece of potato parchment that Polly or Bic (or anyone) had ever seen. It was at least twenty feet long, approximately two feet wide, and nearly filled to the end with Jack of Hearts' neat handwriting.

This letter revealed the truth about Yam Hill.

And the Elders wanted it (and its creator) gone.

25

With the proper potato skin inscription tool, plus a great deal of patience, a person could write very small, fine print on a sheet of potato skin parchment. If you weren't careful, the words (or drawing) you worked so hard to create would smear or become unreadable.

A lot of residents would sometimes keep words (what used to be called taking notes, in Old Earth terminology) when reading an Elder-approved book. And the next time that particular book or magazine came around, you could check them, or reference them, or ponder over what thoughts or ideas you had upon that first reading.

Even Polly's own mother and father would sometimes keep words (notes) when reading their books and magazines. But very few people—possibly no one but Jack of Hearts, or maybe the Three Elders—kept anything close to a daily journal.

Life inside the potato was bland, hardly worth writing down. So even if someone did keep a life journal, it would be filled with tedious descriptions of ordinary things.

But Jack of Hearts' journal, if it was ever read by anyone, would cause a great deal of trouble for those who ruled over the people of the potato. And for everyone inside.

His journal could change lives.

And that could not (and would not) happen. Not under the sovereignty of the Three Elders.

26

"This is what the Three Elders are after," said Jack of Hearts, reaching in and pulling up the great long scroll. "It's not valuable. But it explains everything."

Polly was impressed. "Where did you get a sheet of potato skin that long? I've never seen potato paper like that before."

Jack of Hearts gave a simple answer: "I'm a Digger, Polly, remember? I have access to all the best potato skins, long before the Clothes Makers or anyone else gets their hands on it."

Bic didn't care about the potato skin paper, no matter how long it was. He had plenty of potato skin parchment back in his room. All he was interested in were the strange green claw tools that Jack of Hearts used to dig up his floor. He bent down to pick them up.

"What are these?" Bic asked, holding one in each hand. He clanged them together, enjoying the sound it made. "Did one of the Jewelry Makers invent them?"

The color "green" was familiar to the residents of Yam Hill, but until now it had only been visible in magazines. They looked more reddish in the LED light, but it wasn't hard to tell they were unlike anything he'd ever held in his hands.

"Those were once called a cultivator," explained Jack of Hearts. "They were a kind of gardening tool. In the days of Old Earth, they were used to dig up something called dirt."

Both Polly and Bic had read all about dirt. They'd never seen it or touched it, but knew roughly what it was and what it was supposed to do.

"Dirt is where things like food grows," Jack of Hearts went on. "And trees, and all sorts of plants. And also..." He lifted his head, looking at them both. "Dirt is where potatoes grow. I've seen it."

Polly wanted this to mean that he had seen these things in books or magazines. But she had a startling suspicion that he meant exactly what he had said: that he had seen firsthand that dirt was real. And that would involve going outside. And going outside of Yam Hill was simply not possible. Not unless you were being Ejected.

"Many years ago," said Jack of Hearts, pointing to the Old Earth tool Bic was holding, "those used to belong to Mr. Yamhill, our original founder. I'm not supposed to have them, of course. Let's just say I borrowed them."

"You stole them, didn't you?" Bic let them fall from his hand. He wanted no part of any property that was stolen. "I can't believe I'm getting involved in this. I knew I should've stayed home today."

Jack of Hearts looked away. "Like I said, there are many things going on inside Yam Hill that neither of you understand. Not yet, anyway."

Seated on the floor, Jack of Hearts leaned his back up against a large pile of broken furniture. Polly was thankful that he seemed more relaxed, less likely to completely lose his mind.

"Polly?"

"Yes, Jack?"

"What I said to you before about explaining things when the time was right..." Jack of Hearts stared at her for a long time. "Now is the time. It's all in here, written down. I knew I would have to tell you the truth someday. And since I might not be around much longer..."

"Please don't say that," Polly told him. Losing her friend, even to a natural death, was unthinkable. "You're not going anywhere. You can come and live with us, with my family, if you need to. But you're not going anywhere. I want you to promise me that, okay?"

Jack smiled with his slightly orange but straight teeth, though he refused to promise.

"Thank you for the offer, Polly," said Jack of Hearts, "but there is no hope for me. The Elders know I can no longer be trusted to keep their secrets. Two days ago, they found me a replacement. They tried to Eject me quietly, without anyone knowing about it. But I escaped."

For Bic, it was all beginning to make more sense.

"So that's why you were hiding up in the ceiling?" Bic said. "Because you were supposed to be Ejected two days ago for your crimes, right?"

Jack of Hearts nodded.

"The Elders could be on their way right now, for all I know," Jack of Hearts admitted. "I've got a few friends in the area keeping watch for me. They will signal me if they hear any word that someone is coming this way."

Polly was beginning to think that it may have been a good idea if she had stayed home. She loved Jack of Hearts, loved him like he was family. But this situation was clearly beyond her control.

"From now on, please be careful what you say to your parents," Jack of Hearts said, looking back and forth between the two of them. "That goes for both of you. I don't want any of them getting involved. Your whole family could be in danger."

"My parents?" Polly was suddenly alarmed. "What about them? What do they have to do with all this?"

"My parents don't even know where I am right now," Bic said, inching his way towards the front entrance. "So maybe I better head back home now..."

"It's all in here," Jack of Hearts told them, his big hands holding onto the potato scroll. "Our history. How this place came into existence. All of it. I want you, Polly— and you, Bic—to find a safe place for this journal. Then read it as soon as you can. It's not all word for word, just what I could remember. Maybe one day you can read the actual words for yourself—written down by Mr. Yamhill himself, the creator of Yam Hill."

"That's it," Bic said, shaking his head. "I've heard enough of this. This man is hiding things, and stealing things, and hiding from people…" He was so angry that he couldn't think straight. "We shouldn't be here, Polly. Not one second longer. We're leaving. Come on, before it's too late."

Polly agreed. It was time to go.

"Polly, I want you to take this." Jack of Hearts handed her the long potato skin scroll, which she tucked under one arm. Suddenly, Jack of Hearts reached out one long arm and grabbed hold of Bic, forcing him to come closer. "I want both of you to read this. Promise me, okay? Then you'll know the truth."

"I promise," Polly said.

"Fine," Bic said. "I promise, too. Now let's go, Polly. It's time for us to go home."

That was no longer an option.

They'd had every opportunity to leave. But their chance for escape had come and gone. Now there was someone outside, rattling the front curtain.

Jack of Hearts' warning system had failed.

"JACK OF HEARTS!" said a loud voice. "We know you are in there! Come out into the hallway this very moment and deliver yourself over to us! You have caused great injustice to the people of Yam Hill. And for that, you must be punished to the full extent of our laws!"

Everyone in the room was too afraid to move.

They were trapped.

If the person shouting—and everyone knew exactly who it was, for no one in all of Yam Hill had a voice as loud as his—had simply stuck his head through the front curtain, he would've seen all three of them standing there, eyes open wide, hearts full of fear.

"We all know you are in there, Jack of Hearts," said the First Elder, whose normal speaking voice was nearly as loud as someone shouting. "You know very well why we are here. Amadeus is here with us, so there is no possible escape. Wherever you have been hiding, that is all over now. There is nowhere you can possibly go. You might as well give up. And if there is anyone else in there with you..."

Bic had never once held Polly's hand. After hearing this threat, he immediately grabbed onto Polly's hand and squeezed, painfully hard. And if Polly hadn't been equally as scared, she might've screamed out loud because of the sharp pain he was causing in her left hand. If either one of them dared make a sound, the Three Elders—and somebody called Amadeus—would capture and punish them too, not just Jack of Hearts.

Jack of Hearts had to think fast.

"I am..." He hesitated, then hollered: "I'm using the waste room!" Jack of Hearts cupped his hands together, in order to give the impression of being in another room. "Just give me a moment to finish up, then I'll come with you. I will surrender without fighting or resistance. Just give me a moment to clean up."

Silence followed.

Then more shouting.

"You have one potato minute!" hollered the First Elder. "Then we are coming in. Do you understand?"

"Yes, I understand!" Jack of Hearts shouted back, all the while quickly and quietly ushering Polly and Bic underneath a large pile of destroyed potato furniture.

Polly angrily mouthed the words "no" and "somewhere else." For the life of her, she couldn't understand why Jack of Hearts wanted them to hide out in the open. They'd be discovered the moment the Three Elders stepped into the room.

"I am tired of waiting!" hollered the First Elder, then without warning his large, 6'4 body stepped through the front curtain right as Polly pulled her foot underneath a large section of potato skin.

All three Elders, plus a large bearded Digger named Amadeus, surged into the main room. They paid no attention to the mess, destruction, and complete disarray of his home. No need, since they were the ones responsible.

Polly and Bic lay absolutely still.

"Where are you?" demanded the First Elder. He was standing hardly five or six feet away from Bic and Polly.

Bic didn't know it, but one corner of his potato skin covering was sticking out, clearly visible to anyone who happened to look down.

"I'm in here!" said Jack of Hearts. His muffled voice came from the waste room just around the corner. "Just let me finish tying my covering. Then I'll be right out."

"Fine, fine," said the First Elder. "Just make it fast. I have run out of patience for you, Jack of Hearts."

Polly slid her hand just an inch or two forward, in order to grab Bic's hand. Then she closed her eyes and wished, which was the equivalent of praying in the days of Old Earth. She wished with all her heart, all her mind, to not be seen. She'd never wished so hard for anything in all her life. Bic was doing the same thing right next to her, lying on his stomach, trying not to move, trying to control his breathing, worried that some part of his body may be exposed.

Jack of Hearts would do his best to protect them.

"Greetings to you all, Elders," said Jack of Hearts, coming out of the waste room. "Hello, Amadeus."

As soon as Jack of Hearts stepped into the main living room, he was immediately cornered by the First, Second, and Third Elder, along with his good friend and digging partner, Amadeus.

"Hello, Jack of Hearts," said Amadeus. "We've been looking for you for two days now. I guess I didn't kill you when I was stabbing all those holes into your walls. After a while, we all thought that maybe I did poke a hole in your body while you were hiding like a scared child, and that maybe you were bleeding to death inside your very own walls."

"No," said Jack of Hearts to his old digging crew partner. "You missed. But that's typical for you, isn't it? I've tried to teach you for months how to dig a perfectly round tunnel, or a square tunnel, or how to carve out a perfect piece of potato skin on the first try. But you always discover some new way to fail, don't you?"

Amadeus smiled, if you could call a nearly toothless grin a smile.

"I won't miss this time," said Amadeus. "This time I brought something with me. The Elders said I could have it. I haven't tried it yet, but I think I'll test it on you."

His ex-employee and friend was carrying an Old Earth tool, called a rifle.

27

In the days of Old Earth, handguns and pistols, and all other manner of guns contributed to a large percentage of the total deaths of human beings. Nothing compared to the loss of life that occurred during the Great Unexpected Tragedy, but still enough to be a great concern back then.

Since the creation of Yam Hill, gun violence had dropped to zero.

Guns were something only read about in books. As far as the 604 residents of the potato were concerned, guns or any kind of shooting weapon no longer existed.

But today, after what the Elders always declared as "many hundreds and hundreds of years of civility and peace…" the perfect record of no gun deaths was about to be tarnished.

28

Jack of Hearts remained calm, almost relaxed. He knew that eventually he would be caught. What these men planned on doing with him was the question.

"We finally tracked you down, Jack of Hearts," said the Third Elder, sounding quite cheerful.

Jack of Hearts looked back and forth between these three obviously well-fed, heavyset men. Although the First Elder was much older than the Second Elder and Third Elder, by at least twenty-five years or more, he thought it amusing how they all looked and acted so much alike. Living together, working together, and occupying the same closed off living area, year after year, could do that to people.

"Yes, you did, Elder," said Jack of Hearts. "You finally found me."

"You're a hard man to find," said the Second Elder, wagging a finger at him, a smile on his round face. "Were you in this room the whole time? You don't have to tell us, of course. I was merely curious."

"I was here the whole time, Elder," Jack of Hearts admitted. "I was hiding. Right up there."

They all looked to where Jack of Hearts pointed, where hardly any holes at all had been viciously stabbed into the wall.

"Damn!" The Third Elder snapped his fingers, disappointed that he hadn't been the one to locate the criminal. "And here I had Amadeus stabbing holes into the correct room all along. I just didn't know how high some of your hiding places might be. I had our new employee jabbing that old decorative sword much too low."

"Sorry I couldn't be more help, Elder," Jack of Hearts said to a man he'd known his entire life, and who now wanted him Ejected from Yam Hill before he caused any more irreparable damage.

Looking at the other two Elders, the Third Elder said, "I did guess the correct room, didn't I? The rest of you were off down the hall, searching all the other rooms. So I win the bet."

"Yes, you were right all along," said the Second Elder. "You seem to always have a knack for finding things out. An aptitude, you might say. Or a propensity, is another way of saying it. And yet another way to say it would be a capacity, your competence, or perhaps—"

"Enough," said the First Elder, cutting him off. "You know how I love to listen to your amazing way with words, Elder, but now is not the time."

The Second Elder was Yam Hill's wordsmith. Contributing to the continual education of the people of Yam Hill, the Second Elder would introduce a new word, or sometimes two new words, during the monthly meetings. That way, the undereducated people of Yam Hill—those who were not strong readers, but good listeners—could hear and sound out at least one new word per month.

"I apologize, Elder," said the Second Elder. "You are correct that this is not the time for an exercise in vocabulary. We are here on some rather unusual business."

"Yes, we are," said the First Elder, never taking his eyes off Jack of Hearts. The most powerful man in all of Yam Hill looked disappointed, almost sad.

Jack of Hearts offered a weary smile. "Well, Elders? I'd offer you all a place to sit, but all my furniture has been smashed to pieces."

On a normal day, Jack of Hearts would've loved to have this much company. Today was anything but normal.

"Yes, such a terribly sad day," said the First Elder, who had known Jack of Hearts since he was a baby, and had even helped to raise him. He was the one who had declared a vote to the other Elders, petitioning to bring the then sixteen, or possibly fifteen-year-old Jack of Hearts into their group, allowing him into their world, sharing in things that only the Elders have ever known.

Even though well over twenty years of faithful service had passed since then, it was his recent actions that had brought about the termination of his employment. And soon, an end to his life.

"Sad day indeed, Elder," said Jack of Hearts. He had no intention of stalling, or attempting to prolong his life. If he was to be Ejected, which he knew was coming, he wanted it over with quickly. That would force everyone out of his room and give Polly and Bic enough time to escape and get back home. And then begin the process of forgetting they had ever known the man called Jack of Hearts.

Amadeus held up a pair of hardened potato skin shackles.

"You don't have to put me in potato shackles," said Jack of Hearts. "I can just break through them. Any man with even a small amount of strength in his arms can break them easily enough."

"Yes, we are all aware of that," said the First Elder. "Those potato skin hand-links we have are barely strong enough to restrain a child. They are merely for show, not for actual restraint. No, we won't need them. Unless..."

"Unless what, Elder?" Jack of Hearts asked.

The First Elder stared hard at Jack of Hearts, trying to read his face.

"Not unless there is someone else hiding in here with you," said the First Elder, one bushy orange eyebrow rising into a tall arch. "Young Polly, whom you are so very attached to, for example…"

"There is nobody here but us, Elder," said Jack of Hearts, practically snarling his words. He was attempting to make it perfectly clear that his home had been ransacked once already, and it did not need to happen again. Everything had been destroyed the first time, so any more damage would be a waste of time.

"Go ahead, destroy my home a second time," said Jack of Hearts, swinging his arms out wide. "No one except the four of you has been up here to visit me lately. Believe me…don't believe me. I don't care anymore. There is no one else here, Elder."

His passionate plea was taken seriously.

"I do believe you, Jack of Hearts," said the First Elder. "And yet I wonder what you might have told young Polly over the course of these many years, after so many visits, with the two of you building a friendship together, building up trust."

"Yes, what does she know?" asked the Second Elder. "All of us here in this room—except, of course, for young Amadeus—know precisely about the special bond between you and Polly. We are the ones who helped you in your saddest, darkest days, remember? We fixed what ailed you—loneliness."

There was no sense in denying it.

At a time in his life, somewhere in his mid-twenties, with a good job—two good jobs, one as a digging crew lead with as many as fifty people working under him, on top of his job working for the Elders—he had become desperately lonely. Besides loving his work, and his work companions, he ended up hating the fact that he had only a large, empty living space to come home to, night after night. In a dark depression, Jack of Hearts had gone to the Elders to ask for their help.

And they helped him.

"The First Elder helped me," Jack of Hearts reminded them, his voice less angry. "Not you two. Remember, I was elected Chief Digger of Yam Hill when the two of you were still young men. Both of you were selected only because of two sudden Elder deaths, and because of your relation to original members of Yam Hill."

"I'm afraid you are missing the point," said the Third Elder, the youngest of them all. He was also concerned. "Young Polly is one of the most curious young people currently living inside Yam Hill. I've met her on several occasions. She is wise for her age, very adventurous— same as you, Jack of Hearts. If you have revealed anything to her, now is the time to tell us."

Narrowing his eyes, Jack of Hearts said, "She has nothing to do with this, Elder. You know that I would never bring a child into this. Especially her. That much I promise."

Amadeus made a noise, interrupting the Second Elder when he'd been about to ask Jack of Hearts something else.

"The promise of a dead man?" said Amadeus. "What is that worth? It's not worth one slice of yam, I say."

Although they had worked closely together these last few months—following a recent transfer from another digging crew—this was the first time Amadeus had set foot inside the home of Jack of Hearts, the man whom he had befriended, then turned over to the Elders. This was his first assignment for the Elders. This was also the first time he had interrupted one of the Elders in public, and the Elders did not like to be interrupted.

"Be quiet, Amadeus," said the First Elder without looking at him. And the way he said it caused the new employee to lower his head and apologize.

"Sorry, Elder."

The First Elder locked eyes with Jack of Hearts, who was once trusted, but had since destroyed that trust, and thereby forfeited his life.

"I promise you, Elder," said Jack of Hearts, pleading with his hands and his eyes. "Polly has absolutely nothing to do with this. Besides, I haven't seen her in a week or more. She's been busy with that boy, Blink, or whatever that friend of hers is called."

After a long, uncomfortable silence, the Elders all seemed to relax. Not all, but some of the tension in the room had diffused.

"Very well, Jack of Hearts," said the First Elder. "You spared a young girl's life."

Jack of Hearts thanked him, repeatedly.

Now only his punishment remained.

"Well, Elders?" said the Third Elder. "I, for one, am getting hungry. So why don't we wrap this up, then head back home for a nice meal. I'm in the mood to cook. Today, I think I will make us all a nice lunchtime meal after we finish up here."

"You always did work better on a full stomach, Elder," said Jack of Hearts with a large, fake smile. Telling jokes was not part of his demeanor, but right now he would do anything to change the subject and draw attention away from Polly and Bic, who were both doing a wonderful job of lying still at his feet, unmoving, blending into the chaos that used to be a very comfortable and clean main living area.

"Goodbye, Jack of Hearts," said the Third Elder. "It has been a pleasure having you work for us all these years. I am sad to see your employment with us come to such an end." Then he noticed a piece of yam on his jacket and busied himself with wiping it off.

"Yes, goodbye," said the Second Elder, equally distracted. "You were an excellent employee, Jack of Hearts. You did well by us, working very hard under our command. But I think young Amadeus, here, will be a suitable replacement."

The mood inside the room changed when it came time for the First Elder to say his goodbyes. He was clearly the most upset of all the Elders.

"I have known you, Jack of Hearts, since the day you first came into Yam Hill," said the First Elder. "I can say with absolute certainty that I will miss you. But what you've done cannot be undone. And for that you must be punished."

Jack of Hearts nodded, wisely agreeing with the men who were about to kill him, to send him outside, where very few people knew what it was like.

"Is now the right time, Elder?" asked Amadeus. He was ready to get this over with too. He knew he was going to love being the one to carry out this grim assignment. This was his first ever Ejection.

Over the course of his lifetime, Amadeus had witnessed three Ejections, but had never been actively involved in the process. He could still remember standing on the long potato staircase as a child, trying to peek between the adults, his legs getting tired from all the standing, hardly able to make out what anybody was saying. It surprised him how little emotion he felt knowing that his first Ejection was for his good friend, whom he had turned over to the Elders for the high crime of betrayal, what in the days of Old Earth was called treason.

Today's Ejection was going to be different.

The circle of men surrounding the criminal became tighter and tighter, creating less and less room for a last-minute escape.

Jack of Hearts briefly thought about making one last run for freedom. Living out the rest of his days in hiding was still an option, sneaking around all the hundreds or even thousands of unused rooms inside Yam Hill. Not a pleasant or comfortable life, but still life.

Self-Ejection was always an option, too.

There were many cases throughout the long history of Yam Hill where potato residents, whether they were sick of the loneliness of their lives, sick of the isolation, or even tired of the same food day in and day out, took it upon themselves to make the long and lonely journey up the long flight of potato steps—all 2,080 of them—and simply fling, drop, or crawl out of out of the Ejection site, never to be heard from again.

Jack of Hearts was not any of these things. He wasn't particularly lonely, he didn't feel isolated, and he wasn't even tired of the food.

His heart was sick.

Sick of all the lies.

29

People who had spent their entire lives inside the soft orange comfort of Yam Hill were not accustomed to pain. Slapping a person's face, or punching, or two people fighting as a spectator sport, these were all Old Earth traditions, no longer practiced.

For residents of Yam Hill, actual physical pain caused by someone else was as foreign as the world outside.

30

Polly was tough.
Bic was not.

31

As tough as she might have been, having been instructed to be this way over the years—by Jack of Hearts, the toughest and bravest person she knew—even Polly could hardly take the pain of a nearly 350-pound Elder stepping on her shoulder, sometimes her neck.

The Third Elder remained there for entirely too long. Polly thought the pain would never end.

32

Bic was also in a great deal of discomfort. And yet, unless he wished to be the next in line to be Ejected, he had to remain silent while the struggle raged on above his head.

Thankfully, the person standing on his ribcage was crushing the air out of his lungs. Otherwise he would've screamed, thereby giving themselves away.

33

Jack of Hearts allowed Amadeus, once his good friend and co-worker, to rough him up a bit. Resisting meant they might trip, or fall, and thereby expose the two young residents he was trying so hard to protect.

"My last day is here. To the 2,080 steps it is," said Jack of Hearts, attempting to keep the focus on him and his Ejection. "My final walk inside the hallways of Yam Hill. Despite what you all think, I will miss this place. But if we're going to make it before most people wake up, we should start walking, Elder. This early, there shouldn't be too many people in the hallways."

The First Elder smiled an awkward sort of smile. Jack of Hearts immediately became suspicious. This was a knowing smile, one that insinuated that perhaps they knew something he didn't. His first thought was that they had already uncovered his deepest, darkest, most ambitious secret.

"No, not today," said the First Elder. "You are going to be Ejected, Jack of Hearts, that much I can assure you. But we will not be going to the usual Ejection site. Not when there is no need to travel any further than this very room."

The other two Elders, Amadeus as well, were all grinning, as if they too knew about this dark secret the First Elder was hinting at.

Jack of Hearts could already guess what they had discovered: his secret digging project.

"The proper Ejection site is at least an hour's walk from here, not including all those steps," the First Elder went on. "At my age, I prefer to walk up staircases only when I absolutely have no choice. There is no need to walk all that way." That smile again. "Not when we have an Ejection site right here."

Amadeus aimed the rifle.

"You mean…" Jack of Hearts was at a loss for words. "You know?"

"About your secret exit from Yam Hill?" asked the Second Elder. "Of course we know! There aren't many secrets that can be kept from the Elders…at least not for very long. Though you did manage to keep this one a secret for quite some time."

"And right out in plain view," said the Third Elder, clearly impressed. "Very brave of you, I must say, to maintain this unapproved expansion right in the direct sight of others."

"Lot of work involved," said the Second Elder.

"Yes, a lot of digging," the Third Elder agreed.

Amadeus took the rifle away from his target's face just long enough to point to a spot above the shoulders of Jack of Hearts. The secret exit was roughly six feet up, hidden behind one of Polly's old art projects she had made for him when she was much younger, no older than five, maybe six, or possibly as young as two or three years old.

"There," said the Third Elder. "Behind that child's potato carving. There lies a secret that could easily destroy what we—the other Elders and I, and the Elders before that—have worked so hard to protect."

The one who created it did not need to look where his accusers were pointing. Jack of Hearts had spent several hours a day, most days, creating his own secret escape—a private exodus from Yam Hill.

"We all discovered your secret tunnel purely by accident," explained the First Elder.

"You discovered it, number one," said the Third Elder. "A bit of excellent guesswork on your part, Elder."

"Imagine hiding such a thing in the front room of your own living area," said the Second Elder, sounding equally impressed. "Discovery of that tunnel probably would've gone unnoticed for a thousand years—if, that is, you hadn't begun to spread lies about us, forcing us to come up here and search you out."

"I, myself, have been in this room dozens of times over the years," said the First Elder. "Sat down for a meal right next to that picture. Never once did I suspect anything. Well done, Jack of Hearts. Or well concealed, I should say."

There was no lie big enough to hide the truth. Jack of Hearts didn't want to lie, not anymore.

"But the tunnel I made is not a proper Ejection site," said Jack of Hearts, showing his first signs of resistance. "You can't send me out that way. It may lead to the outside, but there's no telling where it goes. It could be a thousand-foot straight drop!"

All Jack of Hearts knew was that the final section of potato skin had fallen away, along with a loud mess of outside debris—a small landslide.

And when he stuck his hand out...

Cool air.

"Ejection can sometimes mean new life, Elder," said Jack of Hearts, now visibly upset. "You know that as well as I do. But this?" He pointed at Polly's old art project, behind which was an unlit, claustrophobic, nearly six-hundred-foot tunnel. "This tunnel is completely untested. Even I don't know what's on the other side."

"That is not our concern, Jack of Hearts," said the First Elder. "You created that escape. And now, right now, today, you will find out exactly what is out there."

The circle tightened.

Wisely, Jack of Hearts resisted fighting back. Instead, he allowed these four men to corner him, closing in on his secret tunnel and away from the broken pile of potato furniture.

"You can't do this!" shouted Jack of Hearts when the first pair of hands grabbed him. "You can't—"

The barrel of the gun in his face cut him off.

"Quiet!" yelled Amadeus. "You're getting what you deserve, Jack of Hearts."

"YOU CAN'T DO THIS!" the prisoner shouted.

"Of course we can!" the Second Elder told him. "We can do what we like, you fool of a man. We are the highest law of Yam Hill."

Whatever secret Jack of Hearts had stumbled across or discovered, Polly knew it had to be so terrible, so dark, that the Three Elders would do anything—up to and including an illegal Ejection—to keep it a secret.

34

The First Elder gave the order.

All four men grabbed and lifted Jack of Hearts clear off his feet. A bit of a struggle slowed them down. Not because of resistance from the Ejectee, who did not struggle at all, but because such a large man was being lifted up, then stuffed into a very small hole that was at least six feet off the soft, potato floor.

"My goodness, he's heavy!" said the Second Elder as he pushed and shoved, using his shoulder.

This was Jack of Hearts' last chance. Seconds away from his non-ceremonial Ejection, he had to do whatever it took to warn Polly and Bic about life on the outside.

"At least give me a proper Ejection!" Jack of Hearts yelled in the faces of the Elders. It was all he could think of to give him more time.

The Elders, and Amadeus, ignored him as they all continued to lift, push, and shove the condemned man's heavy body into the dark potato tunnel.

Jack had to think quickly. He had to forget about his upcoming death, and focus on saving two other people.

"The fall won't kill you! But to survive, you must remember to—Ahh!" Jack screamed, then nearly lost consciousness when the end of the rifle came forcefully down on the back of his skull.

"Stop fighting us!" yelled Amadeus. Then he put the weapon back down so he could help lift his old boss, raising him up to the tunnel where he would be forced to crawl towards his death.

"If anyone is Ejected from Yam Hill," Jack shouted, followed by more scuffling. "All they must do is stay low to the ground! And when the—"

Polly heard, and felt, a vicious thump.

It sounded like something very hard slammed into the wall.

"That's it!"

"A little more…"

"PROTECT THEIR HEADS!" shouted Jack of Hearts. "Then climb down to the bottom!" More yelling, then: "Why are you hitting me?"

"Help us, then!" shouted one of the Elders.

"Stop fighting us so much!" came another strained voice.

Jack of Hearts was halfway into the tunnel. His words were being swallowed up by the tunnel, just like the rest of his body.

"Go to the yellow house!" came Jack of Hearts' strained voice. "There is enough food there! And water!"

Another crack on the skull.

"Enough of that!" shouted the Second Elder, whose ear was right in the way of all the shouting. "Be a man of courage! Die in a peaceful manner, Jack of Hearts!"

"There he goes..."

"Just a little more..."

The heavy footsteps of four grown men trampling on the broken potato furniture that Bic and Polly were hiding under left them dangerously close to being exposed. Polly got both her arms and one shoulder stepped on, while Bic lost count of how many times he was stepped on, full force, by people who were attempting to Eject someone without a trial, and without letting anyone know. This was Bic and Polly's first insight that anything illegal ever went on inside their beloved Yam Hill.

"Almost there, gentlemen," said the Second Elder, sounding winded but optimistic.

"Now the lower body," said the Third Elder, also struggling. He found it much easier to use his shoulder to push and assist with this unpleasant task.

In time, the accused was fully inside the tunnel.

"Well..." said the Second Elder, breathing hard. "That's...over with. That young man is much heavier than he looks."

The First Elder nearly lost his temper.

"I urge you to use careful words, Elder," said the First Elder, hiding his face. They could all sense he was having a harder time with this than he had previously stated.

The Second Elder apologized.

"Apology accepted," said the First Elder, regaining his composure.

Their work was still incomplete.

After poking his head inside the tunnel, seeing his old crew lead's body there, still moving around, but not crawling down his self-made tunnel towards his death like he was supposed to...

Amadeus fired the rifle.

"ENOUGH!" shouted the First Elder. He covered both ears with his hands, same as the other two Elders. Their faces, wondering what damage the weapon had caused, were both horrified and curious. All of them had read many articles related to guns, and rifles, but had never been around one that was actually fired. And they'd certainly never seen the damage a fired bullet could do to a human body.

"Hmm," said Amadeus. "I missed."

Amadeus has missed his target by more than a foot. And yet the nearly toothless smile on his face was immense, spreading from one undersized orange ear to the other. He had never felt such power. Not even when he was swinging a brand-new potato pick-axe and bringing it down on a soft section of yam.

Both Polly and Bic's bodies jerked when the explosion went off. They'd never heard such a loud noise, or anything close to it.

It terrified them both.

Thankfully, the blast was not loud enough that Polly (or Bic) screamed and gave themselves away. There was so much going on that nobody noticed Bic's right leg slip out from underneath the pile of yam, then quickly disappear again.

"Everyone rest for a moment," suggested the First Elder, still struggling a bit to breathe. Being the eldest Elder, by nearly three decades, he was perhaps in the most pain. His left hand gripped his chest, where a sharp throbbing pain had erupted during the struggle, but was slowly beginning to subside.

"Yes, rest a moment," agreed the Second Elder.

Stuffing the traitor into the tunnel took a great deal of effort from everyone involved. In fact, none of the Elders could remember the last time they'd exerted this much physical activity, unless it was with Ms. Doppelganger.

"Our work is done," said the Third Elder. "But someone, one of us, should stay behind to make sure he doesn't..." His words trailed off.

"I will stand guard," said the First Elder. Holding his hand out, he signaled to Amadeus to hand over the rifle.

Reluctantly, Amadeus handed over the Old Earth weapon. The rifle had been entrusted to him, and carrying it was one of his new responsibilities. He had been an employee of the Elders for only a short time, and already his privileges were being taken away.

"And to prove to the rest of you that I will stay true to my word and not allow the prisoner to return," said the First Elder, followed by a terrible coughing fit.

Everyone waited while the First Elder finished catching his breath. Even in the dim light of the LEDs, it wasn't hard to tell that he was sweating profusely. He did not look well, not at all, and was using the potato wall to stabilize himself.

"Amadeus?" said the First Elder, sounding much more like himself.

"Yes, Elder?" said Amadeus, who was now standing next to the other two Elders.

"I want you to barricade the exit," commanded the First Elder. "Pick up some of this mess here—" He pointed roughly to the area where Polly and Bic were still hiding. "Cover the hole so there is no chance of escape."

"Unless he eats his way through..." Amadeus mumbled.

"What did you say?" asked the First Elder.

"Nothing, Elder," said Amadeus, then he quickly began scooping up piles of yam and stuffing them into the hole.

"Trap him inside, good and tight," said the First Elder, making sure the ambitious new employee was doing his job properly.

"GET MOVING DOWN THERE!" Amadeus shouted into the dark hole.

"There will be no need for that, Amadeus," said the Third Elder, followed by his large stomach growling so loud that it was heard across the room. "Jack of Hearts, I assure you, has accepted his fate and is at this very moment inching his way down that tunnel. He is a good man, faithful to do his part. That much I can assure you." He made sure to acknowledge the First Elder.

Polly and Bic both lay as still as a potato while Amadeus worked hard to block the exit.

More than once they both felt a hand next to their body, perhaps even fingers scraping across their potato skin coverings.

"Is that..." Amadeus was now out of breath. "Is that enough?" Hardly an armful or two more and some part of Bic or Polly's body would be exposed, depending on which pile he reached for next.

Narrowing his eyes at the abrasive young man, the First Elder thought a moment, wanting to choose his words carefully. Amadeus flinched at the way the First Elder was staring him down. Although much, much older, the First Elder was still a good 2-3 inches taller than him.

"At all times, you will address me—" The First Elder stopped. "You will address each of us as Elder. Do you understand? Jack of Hearts had no problem addressing us in such a manner. Do you?"

"No, sir. I mean, no, Elder." Amadeus understood that not only was his job at stake, but perhaps more.

Especially under this stressful situation, which the First Elder was handling remarkably well.

Over near the front curtain, the Second and Third Elder busied themselves with nothing, such as looking around, when all they wanted to do was leave.

"Is that enough, Elder?" said Amadeus, correcting himself and (hopefully) the situation. "I can do more if you would like, First Elder." Even though he had been employed only a short while, he could easily tell he was going to get along much better with the other two Elders.

"That is plenty," said the First Elder.

Amadeus took the hint to step away. He joined the other Elders near the front entrance. There was nothing more for them to do here.

"The three of you can head back home," said the First Elder. "I will finish up here and make sure my dear Jack of—" He did not catch himself in time. The others caught his mistake, but made no comment. "That is, I mean to say that I will make sure the Ejected resident does not return. That he stays Ejected."

"What will you say if anyone shows up?" asked the Second Elder. "What if one of his digging crew members arrives here, looking for him? Or asks questions as to why you are here? Or about this mess?"

The First Elder responded, "Lie, Elder. I will explain that Jack of Hearts is simply not here. I will tell them, or anyone else that may show up, that I merely came all this way to visit, and that I too found him gone."

"And if Polly shows up?" asked the Second Elder, approaching the subject delicately.

"I will tell her the same thing," replied the First Elder.

"Will she believe you?" asked the Third Elder.

The First Elder said, "Polly is a child, still in her teenage years. Young people believe what they are told, Elder." Turning his back on them all was signal enough that it was time for them to leave. Which they did, quickly leaving the room and heading down the dim hallway, back to their well-lit and well-fed lives.

The First Elder lingered, hesitant to leave.

The next few minutes felt like an eternity for those wishing to stretch out their contorted bodies.

Standing at the front exit, peering around the room one last time, the First Elder said his silent goodbyes to Jack of Hearts, who may already be close to the end of his long tunnel, and possibly already discarded himself.

One last bit of closure was to turn off the lights.

The First Elder pulled one tiny red LED light from the wall near the front exit, then dropped it to the floor and crushed it into the soft potato floor with a polished Old Earth dress shoe that was just his size.

The whole room turned black.

Jack of Hearts' home would remain forever dark.

"Goodbye, my son," said the First Elder, softly, but still loud enough to be heard.

Then he too was gone.

35

Fear is an emotion not often experienced inside the protective orange walls of Yam Hill. Residents can experience nervousness, perhaps anticipating some news about a family member, or a friend, or even about attending the monthly Community Meeting.

Residents may experience anxiety, maybe after running into an old friend in the hallway after several years of not visiting, despite their many invitations. Or even excitement, perhaps after finally receiving a long-awaited Old Earth magazine or book in the mail.

But to be truly fearful was extremely rare.

Polly and Bic had now both experienced it. Fear that their young potato lives were about to come to an unforeseen end.

36

Same as it was during the days of Old Earth, time seemed to pass more slowly for someone in distress. And the more discomfort being experienced, the slower time seemed to move. Sometimes the experience was so bad that time could give the illusion of stopping completely.

When a person is lying in an uncomfortable position for an extended period of time, bent and twisted—especially when they've eaten nothing but potatoes their whole life, causing the muscles to weaken due to lack of Iron and protein—each passing second could feel like an eternity.

Both hideaways were suffering in silence.

Polly and Bic (Polly especially) were at the point where an Ejection sounded like a suitable alternative to their current suffering.

The pain was becoming unbearable. And if it lasted much longer, Polly did not care about the consequences. She would scream, quite loud.

37

"Bic?" Polly whispered. Her words came out so quietly that she was certain they went unheard. Either that, or completely ignored. And justifiably so, done out of genuine fear for his life.

"Bic?" she said a bit louder. "I have to move. I can't lie here like this anymore. My leg feels like it's going to walk off on its own."

No answer. Not even a signal, or a hand squeeze.

If anyone was still in the room with them, Polly was certain that by now she would've felt a strong pair of hands reach into the pile of potato mess they were hiding in, grab her by the hair, or whatever else they could grab, then rip her violently to her feet. By now, she was in so much pain that she felt it was worth the risk to move, to get the blood flowing again.

"I think they're gone," Polly said, loudly this time. Loud enough so that she knew he heard. No hand reached in to grab her, which was great news.

"Bic?"

There was no way Bic could've fallen asleep. But knowing him, perhaps she was wrong. It felt like it'd been hours since Jack of Hearts shoved them under here, buried them, covered them up in a final attempt to protect them from the Elders. It had been his dying effort.

As soon as Polly made the slightest move, Bic squeezed her hand, tight, meaning *no, don't move.*

Polly spoke in her regular voice. "Bic, if I don't move soon, I'm going to scream. And if I scream, we're going to get caught anyway, so—"

As if on its own accord, Polly's right leg straightened.

"Much better." Polly was absolutely in love with the sensation of blood re-entering her tingling legs. She stretched out her left leg, followed by both her arms. After feeling life (and blood) returning to parts of her body where circulation had been cut off, she took a real chance and sat up, exposing herself completely.

Large pieces of broken potato furniture fell away to reveal the body of a teenage girl who had just listened in on a conversation that she should not have overheard.

The truth about Yam Hill—parts of it, at least—were now exposed and brought into the dim red LED light they lived by. There was still some darkness yet to be exposed, but Polly was up to the challenge. What they had discovered would have to be revealed to everyone, to all residents of the potato.

The Elders were liars.

Always had been.

Polly had heard the proof with her own ears—from which she was now digging out chunks of cold yam.

"Wake up in there!" Polly said, brushing off chunks of squashed yam and old dried up potato skin. "Bic! It's safe to come out. They're gone. I'm speaking the truth. You can come out now. But the room is completely dark. I think they took all the lights with them when they left. I can still see the light coming from the hallway though, underneath the front curtain."

Still no movement from the overly cautious Bic.

Not until Polly reached down into the pile of yam, felt around, then pinched him as hard as she could, did she finally get a reaction. Being so dark, plus the fact that she had shoved her hand into a random spot, she had no idea where she pinched him, but thought it might've been his stomach.

"Hey!" Bic cried out. Chunks of yam fell away as he sat up. Then he too began picking and wiping off all the excess. "You pinched my hip bone."

"Finally, you listen to me," Polly said. "I thought you fell asleep."

"You're right," Bic said, looking around and seeing absolutely nothing but pitch black. "It is dark in here. Really dark."

The hallway lights, about twenty-five feet away, offered at least a small amount of comfort. Coming out of a dark hiding spot to find only more darkness was an odd (and scary) sensation. This was what Bic imagined being Ejected was like: Being thrown out into complete darkness, a gruesome death on its way, but still alive for the time being.

"Good thing the hallway lights are still on," Bic said. "Otherwise it might take us a long time to find our way out of here."

"I'd get us out of here," Polly said, attempting to stand up. Although her first attempt failed, causing her to plop back down on their pile of broken yam furniture, her second attempt went much smoother. Her legs and most of her lower body were experiencing paresthesia, what was called "pin-and-needles" back in the days of Old Earth.

"Yes, I'm sure you could," said Bic, who did a much better job of standing up than Polly. He managed on the first try, even with a very stiff back and several bruised (or possibly dislocated) ribs.

"You've spent probably half your life up here," Bic went on, not exaggerating in the least. "I'll bet you know your way around here just as well—or better—than your own home."

"Yes, you're probably right," Polly told him.

"Can you believe what just happened?" Bic said. Then, clearly not thinking, he said, "That was the wildest, the craziest thing I've ever known!" He sounded almost excited, even exhilarated. "I mean, they Ejected him Polly. The sent him outside!"

"Quiet your voice down, Bic. Please." Polly's words silenced him. But Bic was right. It was the wildest, craziest thing that had ever happened in her life, or Bic's. And it all happened within the last twenty minutes, hardly a dozen steps from where they now stood.

"I'm sorry, Polly," Bic said. "I didn't mean to say it that way. Me and my foolish words. I'm sorry, Polly."

"It's okay, Bic. Forget it."

"No, it's not okay, Polly," Bic told her. "Jack of Hearts is gone, and it's not fair. Don't you dare think for one potato minute that what happened here was your fault, okay? There was nothing we could do, Polly."

Polly nodded, but Bic could tell he wasn't getting through. She was already blaming herself. Or if she wasn't doing so now, it was only a matter of time.

"Those were the Elders, Polly," Bic went on. "All three of them, plus that Amadeus man—he scares me. There was no way we could've put up a fight. Even if we dared to try, they would've captured us, too. And we're just kids. What can a couple of kids do against four adults? How would we stop them? We did the best we could, Polly. We stayed hidden just like Jack of Hearts wanted us to."

Better, but still not enough to break through.

"Jack of Hearts died to protect us," Bic said. "He died to protect both of us. He was brave right up until his Ejection. He was—he *is* a brave man."

In the dark, Polly felt a hand fumble around and accidently grope her leg before it worked its way up to her shoulder, where it stayed for a moment. Then she felt a hand on each shoulder, right before being pulled in close for a full body embrace.

Polly tried very hard not to cry. Bic squeezed his arms around her, and she squeezed back even harder. It was the only thing she could do to stop herself from breaking down. She would cry later, probably a lot.

Right now, Polly was too angry to cry.

The fact that her best adult friend, Jack of Hearts, had just been unfairly Ejected was a lot to handle. But she was doing her best to stay focused, to remain in control.

Witnessing an Ejection is something that stays with you. Always. Even if the experience came when you were very young, you still understand that Ejection is the worst thing that can happen. And an illegal Ejection would be impossible to forget.

"Polly?" Bic said, now standing beside her.

"Yes?" Polly wiped her eyes in the dark. She had never once cried in front of Bic, so was glad they were standing in near pitch black.

"Did you know he had a secret Ejection site?" Bic asked. "I always knew Jack of Hearts was a great Digger. But, Polly! An Ejection site? He actually dug an exit to the outside world. It must've taken years!"

Polly shook her head. "Jack of Hearts didn't build an Ejection site, Bic. He built an escape—for us." After thinking about it, she added, "I think...yes, I think that was probably what he was going to tell me. Remember what I said about Jack of Hearts coming downstairs to find me? And explaining that he had something important to tell me?"

Bic remembered.

"Now that I think about it," Polly went on, "he was agitated and nervous that last time I spoke to him. I think maybe he knew this was going to happen. That they were going to send him outside."

Bic could've very easily worked his mind into a panic just thinking about it. How horrible it must've been for Jack of Hearts, knowing that he was going to be Ejected.

"Outside is one place I never want to see," Bic said, trying to shake off the very idea. "I can't even imagine how horrible it is out there. The outside world is no place for people. Not anymore. Definitely no place for us."

Polly looked confused.

They'd often spoken about this very thing: *What was outside of Yam Hill?* And all those times, most times, he had seemed excited, almost as inquisitive and curious about Old Earth as Polly.

"You mean you don't want to know what's out there?" Polly couldn't believe it. Now that the outside was actually here, just a few steps to their immediate left, it was suddenly a forbidden subject. It's easy to be brave when the thing you fear is on the other side of Yam Hill. But when it's in the room with you, it's easy to become anxious, even terrified. Polly's mind filled with wonder, thinking how Jack of Hearts must've discovered a new exit, possibly a new world. A New Earth, where people didn't die a horrible death the moment they left Yam Hill.

"The Old Earth is dead, Polly," Bic said, stating a fact. "Everybody knows that. Even little kids know that Old Earth doesn't exist anymore."

"You might know that, Bic—" Polly stopped because she wanted to choose her words carefully. "You might think you know that, but none of us can be sure what's really out there. Maybe Jack of Hearts found a new Old Earth, where not everyone dies the second they leave here. Did you think about that?"

This was all Bic could stand. He hated to yell at his friend, especially since she'd just lost somebody so close to her, but this crossed a dangerous line. What she was talking about—Old Earth, what might possibly still be out there, perhaps even hinting about going outside to check—was absolute madness.

"All I know, Polly," Bic said, "is that I heard one hundred percent fear in your friend's voice." Bic regretted putting it like that, so bluntly, but he wanted to get his point across. And quickly, so she would stop talking like this.

"He was screaming, Polly," Bic continued. "Screaming as if going outside is the worst possible thing that can happen to a person. Which I personally believe it is."

Polly made an exasperated noise.

This was one of the rare times where she found herself on the losing end of an argument. Usually she was the one that made all the good points, but not this time.

She understood his perspective, she truly did. It was just hard for her to accept the fact that her best friend didn't share the same passion, the same wonder, the same curiosity about what could possibly be outside Yam Hill.

In a calmer voice, Polly said, "Well, I don't know what's out there, Bic. I've never been outside. Never even seen outside. How can any of us truly know what's out there? Only people who are Ejected know what's really out there and—"

Polly stopped.

After a long pause, Bic said, "Really what, Polly?"

Polly wanted to answer, but couldn't. Her mouth suddenly twisted up into a fearful expression from what she just saw. Bic's head was turned towards her, so he didn't see the flicker of a shadow that passed by the front curtain. But both of them heard the shuffling sound of someone walking past the main entrance.

Bic let out a soft, desperate moan.

Polly found Bic's rigid body in the dark and quickly grabbed him from behind. One arm reached around his waist, and the other arm snaked its way up and around his neck, where her free hand clamped down over his mouth to prevent him from making another sound.

Breathing in unison, their chests moving in time, the two of them stared, unblinking, in the direction of the front curtain. Each of them expected the curtain to move, followed by a dark figure coming in to grab them.

Several minutes passed with no other sounds.

Neither Polly or Bic dared to say anything, or move even the slightest bit until they were positive, absolutely certain, that whoever it was had gone.

"Probably just someone passing by," Polly whispered after a long silence.

Bic was ready to believe it. That there was nothing threatening out there, and that it had merely been someone passing by in the hallway, perhaps one of Jack of Hearts' friends from the next floor.

"Of course it was," Bic said, confident that they were alone once again. "It was probably just someone on their way to..." Bic did the equivalent of shrugging his shoulders. "To somewhere, I suppose."

"Home?" Polly suggested.

"Yes, exactly," Bic said. "On their way home." By now, he was ready to believe anything just so he could leave this dark room and go back to his moderately lit room, and the safety it provided.

"Probably just one of the neighbors," Bic said. "Right, Polly?"

"Right," Polly said. "Just a neighbor."

"Polly?"

"Yes, Bic?"

"Can we go home now?" Bic asked. "My stomach feels sick."

Polly had never wanted to go home as badly as she did right now. She wanted to see her parents. Maybe she would really surprise them and give each of them a full body embrace, same as the one that Bic had just shared with her.

"Here, take my hand," Polly said, leading the way. "Watch out for the—"

"Sorry!" Bic immediately tripped over a large pile of yam, accidently pulling Polly backwards and nearly dragging them both to the floor.

"It's okay," Polly said, somehow managing to stay upright. "Just go slow, Bic. There's still broken potato furniture all over the place, remember?"

The red light from the LEDs grew brighter as they made the short journey to freedom. Not bright, by any means, but providing enough visibility that they could see where they were stepping.

Relief overcame them both as they stood next to the front curtain. Freedom was just outside those strips of dangling potato skin. Warm red light lit their feet. Both their faces were partially lit through the missing sections of thin potato skin curtain that had been ripped down by the Elders.

Bic poked his head outside just enough to see that the immediate area was clear. Not far enough to see up or down the hallway, only what lay just outside.

"The hallway is empty," Bic said. "Let's get away from this place, Polly."

Before they headed home, Polly wanted to make one thing clear. As Bic was moving towards the hallway, she grabbed him by the hand and made him promise that they would tell everyone what happened, as soon as possible.

"So, the plan is that we go home and tell our parents first," Polly said. "And after that, we tell everybody. Does that sound right to you?"

"What? Wait. Absolutely not," Bic said, pulling back his hand. "I don't think we should tell anyone, Polly. Nobody. Not even our parents. I think we should just go home, maybe get something to eat, and pretend that none of this ever happened. That's the easiest way to deal with this. And the safest, too."

Even though they were still standing next to a recent crime scene, Bic felt this subject should be settled before they went anywhere. Before they even left the room, that's how serious he was about this matter.

"If we start telling people, Polly, then we could be in danger too," Bic said. "What if everyone we tell thinks we're lying? That we're making the whole thing up? Jack of Hearts will still be gone—that's truth. But what's to stop them from saying that he didn't Eject himself? It's happened before, you know. I've heard my parents talk about the Solitaires. They all live alone in almost complete darkness. All of them drink some kind of potato juice that makes them forget things. And when they can't take one more day of living, they Eject themselves."

"Yes, I know about the Solitaires, Bic." Polly didn't see what those sad and lonely people had to do with this situation.

"Well, if you hadn't noticed, Polly..." Bic wasn't sure how to say it without sounding mean, or insensitive. "Jack of Hearts was kind of a Solitaire. No life partner, no children of his own..."

Polly looked away. She was upset because, once again, he was absolutely right.

"It'll be our version of what happened against theirs," Bic went on. "And who do you think everyone will believe, Polly? Us, or the Elders?"

With tears filling up her eyes and threatening to spill down her cheeks, Polly angrily wiped them away.

"They Ejected my friend, Bic," Polly said. "Our friend. He saved us both, remember?" Saying the words out loud, she had to really choke back her tears. Bic sensed it, but he had to keep pushing.

"We need to keep quiet about this," Bic said. "At least for now, okay? Maybe..." He sighed and gave it a second thought. "Maybe when the time is right, we'll tell people what happened here today. That's the best I can do right now, Polly. Now can we please just go home?" He was already halfway outside, his body inching its way into the hallway, towards freedom.

"Fine," Polly said. "Let's go home."

"Polly, I know what you're worried about," Bic told her. "I promise, we'll come back for it some other time, okay? When all this has settled down."

"Come back for what?" Polly asked.

"The letter," Bic said. "Jack of Hearts' letter, of course. The one he wanted you to have."

"He wanted us to have it," Polly told him as she rearranged her potato skin covering, pulling at something underneath. She said no more, other than: "We don't need to worry about the letter."

"We'll come back for it later," Bic said, which surprised her. "Right now, I think we both need to go back home and forget about this. At least until we can sort this out, or come to some kind of agreement about how to handle this. And then, after it's settled, I'll bring up some extra LEDs and we can search for that letter, okay?"

With the front curtain pulled wide open, the red light from the hallway lit up their faces, both of which were still messy and covered in small pieces of yam.

"You have extra LEDs?" Polly asked, though she already knew the answer.

"Well, I kind of..." Bic mumbled some incoherent answer.

"Mm-hm," Polly said. "You went around to some of the unused rooms and stole the LEDs, didn't you? Probably so you can have more reading light."

"Hey, those old Community Rooms are practically never used," Bic said, weakly trying to defend his actions. "And besides, nobody will ever notice them gone, anyway, so there's no harm in me borrowing some extra lights and wire."

"Stealing is an Ejectable offense, Bic," Polly said, teasing him. "I should probably report you." Making a joke was a nice change, a reprieve from their situation and all that had happened.

"Be quiet, you," Bic said, jokingly. "You've got extra LEDs too."

Together, both half-smiling, they left the room and headed out into the hallway, just outside of the dark, empty, destroyed home of the late Jack of Hearts.

Bic said, "Come on, let's go home before—"

That's as far as he got.

"Too late for that," said the First Elder. "Restrain them, Amadeus. Quickly."

38

Not one, but two large bodies blocked the hallway. The First Elder, acting on his instinct, had wisely asked his new employee to wait with him for a while, in the off-chance that Polly, or Bic, or anyone else showed up this morning.

After checking all the other rooms, searching for any evidence of Jack of Hearts making a re-entry into Yam Hill, perhaps through another secret tunnel, those lights had also been shut down. They were about to leave when the First Elder thought he heard voices coming from back inside the main room, which he was certain he'd left dark and empty.

Unexpectedly, the two people the First Elder knew he would have to deal with eventually, Polly and Bic, came walking right out of the main room. Right where an illegal Ejection had taken place only a short while ago.

"And to think you two were in the room all along," said the First Elder, shocked but also relieved that the trespassers had been caught. Having them tell residents what had transpired here, especially seeing as how well-liked Jack of Hearts was throughout the potato community, it could be extremely disastrous for the Three Elders.

"I knew it!" said Amadeus. "I thought I felt something strange when you told me to block off the exit, Elder. When I was scooping up handfuls of yam, picking up pieces of that broken seat, I could've sworn I felt a leg or maybe an arm under there."

Amadeus was back in charge of the rifle.

"I also had a suspicious feeling," said the First Elder, looking back and forth between Polly and Bic, whose faces were overcome with shock. "Why else would Jack of Hearts have shouted all those foolish instructions?"

Amadeus looked confused.

Typically, on any given work day, he took many instructions from his old boss, Jack of Hearts, the man he'd just assisted in Ejecting. But to the best of his knowledge, he hadn't heard the man give any instructions.

"When a body is Ejected from Yam Hill," explained the First Elder, speaking directly to Polly and Bic, "it would not travel in any such downward direction, unlike what Jack of Hearts was declaring to you. The body would travel up."

"What about when they're Ejected illegally, Elder," said Polly, not fully understanding what the Elder meant, but understanding that they were good and caught. And that a good show of anger might be their only way out of this. "What happens then?"

With a pleasant smile and slow movements, Amadeus gently laid the rifle against the wall. Then, faster than Polly thought a large man could move, he grabbed her roughly by the shoulders, picked her up off her feet, and then slammed her up against the potato wall.

Potato floors can be surprisingly soft.

Potato walls can be surprisingly hard.

When Polly's head bounced off the wall, she thought she was seeing what the Old Earth magazines called *sky*. Polly's head was thumping, painfully, and she saw many tiny flashing lights just out of her reach. Residents of Yam Hill lived their entire lives bathed in red light. These tiny flashes were much lighter in color—a color she wasn't quite sure how to describe.

The hallway mood suddenly changed. The First Elder turned on his new employee.

"Do that again, Amadeus," said the First Elder, "and I will personally see to it that your fragile human body is disassembled in Mr. Yamhill's workshop before it is Ejected—in pieces."

Amadeus, the eager new employee, carefully dropped Polly to her feet. Bic tried to help her.

"I apologize for doing that, Elder," said Amadeus, who had a genuine look of surprise on his face. "I thought you wanted me to. I didn't mean to hurt her so bad. I've never actually done that to a person. I didn't know how much force to use, since I've never actually used force for anything—other than digging, I mean."

"Be quiet, Amadeus," said the First Elder. "You will keep your mouth shut and do as I tell you. And right now, I am telling you to apologize to this young lady, who did not deserve that abuse of force."

"Yes, Elder," said Amadeus. "Sorry about that, kid."

Polly was too dizzy to accept his apology. Even if her head wasn't thumping, and she wasn't seeing flashes of bright light, she wouldn't have accepted the apology. Not from either of them. All she wanted was Jack of Hearts back.

When things settled down, the First Elder gently placed his right hand on Polly's left shoulder.

"Polly?" said the First Elder.

Polly gave no reply. She felt drained. All she had left in her was to stare defiantly at the First Elder. It was a look filled with sadness from losing a friend, and anger at the man who took him away.

"What?" she finally said, snapping at the Elder.

"Polly, you will address me as Elder," said the First Elder. "Nothing more, but certainly nothing less."

Polly was completely worn out. She looked up, way up into the First Elder's eyes, which were surprisingly kind just now. Unlike Polly's eyes, seething with hatred behind some fresh tears.

"You just Ejected my friend," Polly said, "and you're mad because I won't call you by your proper name? Jack of Hearts told me ages ago that's not your real name. You all have Old Earth names, just like the rest of us. He didn't tell me what they were, but I know it's true. Jack of Hearts always told me the truth. The complete opposite of all you Elders, who are nothing but a bunch of disgusting liars."

The First Elder's grip on Polly's shoulder relaxed, though he didn't release her completely.

Bic was worried that they might unseal the hole from the secret Ejection site and stuff Polly in there if she didn't watch her words more carefully.

"Polly, just do as he says," Bic told her. Unlike Polly, he regarded the First Elder with a great deal of esteem and admiration.

"You should listen to your friend, Polly," said the First Elder.

Bic smiled, suddenly optimistic that they would be able to talk their way out of this. If Polly kept quiet, he would make the First Elder see reason. And, to the best of his ability, he would make the First Elder realize that they were only young, and how they shouldn't be held accountable for their actions. Then the two of them could go home and never speak of this again.

"Elder?" said Bic.

"Yes, Bic?" said the First Elder.

"This is all just a simple mistake," Bic told him, trying to defuse the deadly situation. "Neither one of us knew anything about what Jack of Hearts did to you. We just came up here for a fast visit. We didn't mean to get involved in this."

"Of course you didn't mean to get involved in this," said the First Elder, nicely enough and with a smile so wide that for a moment Bic thought he might let them go.

Polly didn't believe a word of it.

"Regardless of that, however..." The First Elder reached out his right hand, grabbing onto Polly's potato skin covering just behind the neck, holding on tight with his large hands, so the prisoner could not flee.

"What are you going to do, Elder?" Polly snapped at him. "Eject both of us? Eject two kids?"

The First Elder replied with a simple, "Yes."

But there was more than a hint of sadness behind his eyes, visible even in the dim red glow of the hallway light.

There was one last job to do. Only then could Amadeus and the First Elder go back to their comfortable living quarters, and enjoy the lunch that the Third Elder had promised to cook for them.

"I'm sorry for this, Polly," said the First Elder, squeezing her shoulder, hard. "Rules are rules."

39

In the entire history of Yam Hill, there had never been a Double Ejection. The closest thing to it was just six months ago, when the lovely married couple Mr. and Mrs. Geyser had been Ejected within a week of each other.

This was going to be much different. And the less people that knew about it, the easier it would be to explain during the next Community Meeting.

40

Normal social behavior for residents of Yam Hill dictates that you do not walk (or run) away from somebody that is speaking to you. And you certainly do not run away from an Elder, especially after he has called your name. You stop immediately, and then listen attentively to what he has to tell you.

Bic was too scared to run.

Polly, however, was not too scared to run—though she didn't get far. And she certainly wasn't too scared to shout insults, or yell and scream at the First Elder so loud that it hurt Bic's ears. And she certainly did not restrain from using her arms and legs, throwing wildly uncoordinated kicks and punches as she was dragged down the hallway by her long, orangish-brown hair. She was being led toward the last place that everyone must eventually go.

Old Earth.

Usually, this did not happen within the first fifteen to twenty years of life, when a person's body was at the healthiest stage of life.

"What about the other one?" asked Amadeus, shouting down the hallway to the First Elder, who had his hands full at the moment. "The friend, here, shall I drag him by the hair, too?"

"No, he will follow," the First Elder responded.

Amadeus began to walk after them.

Bic followed.

41

There are no diseases inside Yam Hill. No long-term painful suffering. No communicable viruses that could wipe out an entire family, or spread quickly and kill off an entire section of Yam Hill. Although people sometimes got sick and died, it was due to a prolonged lack of vitamins.

Scientific studies done by people of Old Earth proved that the human body requires approximately 40 different vitamins and nutrients to be healthy. Yam Hill residents were lucky to get a third of those essential vitamins and nutrients.

And despite the deficiencies of a yam only diet, most people's lives turn out to be quite long. Forty, maybe fifty years. Other lives, for various reasons, end up being quite short.

42

The act of "kicking" is done almost exclusively by children. Most often, the practice of pulling back one's leg and then forcefully launching it in a forward arc happens when young residents are engaged in a game of Yam Sphere, the equivalent of kick ball from back in the days of Old Earth.

Children grow tired of action games early in life. By the time they turn eight, or ten, or sometimes as young as five or six, most have lost interest in running, exploring, and games that involve physical activity. They turn to a more sedentary lifestyle, same as their parents.

This is not always the case, since there are a handful of older residents throughout Yam Hill—some in their twenties, thirties, or even forties—who still enjoy kicking around a yam sphere.

Unfortunately, games never last long.

Forming a yam sphere into a playable unit involves wrapping one long continuous potato skin strip into a circular shape, then finding a way to tie a knot to keep it together. This highly time-consuming process is one of the main reasons that children lose interest in Yam Hill's only sport. The amount of actual playing time is hindered, or sometimes halted altogether due to constant repair of the ball, or *sphere*.

Kicking another person, however, is highly irregular.

Kicking and screaming (especially done simultaneously) had never been witnessed by anyone currently living inside the sanctity and quietude of Yam Hill.

This is exactly what many residents of Yam Hill witnessed today: A young lady being dragged by her potato covering, screaming for help, her body thrashing around, completely out of control. All this at the hands of an Elder—possibly the First Elder, though it was too dark to say for certain.

The bodies moved much too swiftly through the dim hallways to tell precisely who it was. Otherwise the face of the child might've been recognized, and the parents alerted.

No one reported this strange event. No one. There was no one to report this to—the Elders were the highest law inside Yam Hill. And since it was an Elder pulling the screaming female resident along with him, surely there was a justifiable reason, so there was no need to get involved.

43

When a body is severely lacking in vitamin D, the skin can bruise quite easily. Even more so with a lack of zinc in the diet. And bioflavonoids. Calcium. Omega-3.

When a person eats nothing but potatoes—even yams, which are high in vitamin E and vitamin A—all it takes is no more than a few pounds of pressure to cause a painful, purplish-black bruise.

Fingernails are also affected. They become weak without enough protein in the diet. Too much vitamin A, which is abundant in yams, can also weaken keratin, the main structure of human hair and fingernails.

Even walls made entirely of yam can rip fingernails right off the hand. When enough force is applied, even the thumbnail can be torn clean away.

44

Loud noises are rare inside Yam Hill. Noise is deadened by the thick orange walls. They soak up the sound so that potato life continues to be lived in a calm and quiet environment.

Cries for help cannot always be heard.

45

Sustenance over variety is the way of life for residents of Yam Hill. This is how lives are lived, with not much in the way of change, but plenty of fiber and potassium to keep a body living.

And this favorite saying of the Three Elders—sustenance over variety—was often quoted during the Community Meetings.

The words were meant to inspire—if not hope, then at least offer a feeling of persistence, that they all must go on living to the best of their ability. That they, the people of the potato, the residents of Yam Hill, the survivors of the Great Unexpected Tragedy, owed it to themselves to go on living. Even if life was bland most days.

Sustenance over variety.

Apathy over truth.

46

By the time the bottom of the Ejection Site staircase was reached, nearly an hour later, Polly felt as if a large percentage of her body had become one giant painful bruise. Especially the wrist she'd been dragged by, her left, and the back of her neck, which had also been used to escort her through Yam Hill.

As they began to climb the 2,080 steps, Polly had run out of energy to fight. She climbed without any further resistance.

This morning, Polly had woken up and wished to go for an adventure. Soon she would be one quick shove away from experiencing an adventure unlike any other. One which every living person must experience, though they are usually not alive when their body is released back to the Old Earth.

The actual Ejection was not the worst part.

A terrible guilt was crushing Polly's insides, weighing down on her like the sheer mass of Yam Hill itself. It hurt significantly more than the brutal grip the First Elder had on her wrist.

The sickening feeling in her stomach, accompanied by the dark thoughts plaguing her young mind, was not because she was only a few steps from being Ejected from Yam Hill. It was because Bic was going with her. She would be Ejected first, and then he would go next.

Each time Polly screamed his name, Bic would reply, "Polly, I'm right here behind you!"

And knowing that it was her fault that Bic was involved in this dreadful mess, that his young life was also about to be extinguished, it made the guilt even more unbearable. But all her critical thinking, all the guilt, it would all end just as soon as she made it to the top.

Just a few more steps…

47

The steps leading up to the Ejection Site have been around almost as long as Yam Hill itself. Within the first three weeks of the Great Unexpected Tragedy, the first window to the outside was created: A simple square-shaped cutout that was carved from the soft inner core, and finally the much tougher outer potato skin.

There was enough room for several people to stand side-by-side, right next to the Ejection site cutout. People could look down upon their old life, what was soon referred to as Old Earth because of the near total loss of human life. And the justified speculation that the planet was no longer habitable.

People had abused the Earth for centuries.

One day, the Earth fought back.

48

In the early days, the staircase was built to be a lookout point, not an Ejection Site. Within a few short months of living inside Yam Hill, things began to change.

Fear of a repeat global tragedy caused fewer and fewer people to make the trip up the staircase, where they could look out at the colorful planet they once enjoyed. What was supposed to be a hopeful, invigorating experience quickly turned into a depressing one filled with feelings of separation, coupled with a longing for the way things used to be.

During the first few months after the global disaster, many tests were implemented by the hopeful ones. The potato residents who wished to return to the Old Earth as quickly as possible. Items were tossed out into the atmosphere, in hopes that the Great Unexpected Tragedy would soon be over, and people could return to their old way of living.

Every single test failed.

The debris alone should've been a clear indicator that things had obviously not returned to normal. For weeks and months these tests went on, until the non-hopefuls—those who had quickly grown accustomed to life inside a giant potato and the safe environment it provided—took a vote to declare that these tests were prolonging not only a sense of false hope, but also a giant waste of valuable Old Earth items that were no longer accessible. Things such as books and magazines, silverware, and paper. What items remained accessible, would remain inside Yam Hill, including every last living human being.

Even those once-hopeful residents adapted to spending all their time inside their potato rooms, carving out a new existence for themselves.

There was much work to do.

Much work.

Hallways were being created at a fantastic pace by the newly formed Digging Crew. Back then, volunteering to be a Digger was at its zenith. It was a work filled with pride for the perseverance of the people of the potato, digging their way to a new kind of life.

Great hollows were discovered. Long stretches where the potato had grown so fast, at such an extraordinary rate, that huge cracks—open areas where nothing grew—could be reformed and reshaped into walkable pathways, or staircases, or an entire new living development.

Further potato expansion led people to move away from the original area. What was once a close-knit community, wherein every family lived within roughly the same hundred meters, was now able to spread out across acres of undeveloped yam.

Lights were set up so that people could travel further and further inside the ever-expanding hallways of Yam Hill. Human eyes adjusted, adapting quickly after spending so much time in the dim red light. This potato technology was introduced by the creator himself, Mr. Yamhill, a retired electrician who once ran his own successful company.

Because of Mr. Yamhill, who in life was an avid reader, his collection of books and magazines began to circulate. People now stayed indoors most of the time, reading, doing what married couples do, or decorating their new potato homes.

Then came the first ever Ejection.

After so much global death, the idea of discarding another human body was almost too much for anyone to bear. Especially given that it would be the funeral for the very man who had so bravely risked his own life to save them—the survivors. The only ones rescued from the strange upwards fate that took the lives of all those billions of fellow men, women, and children.

49

Mr. Yamhill saved fifty-seven people that terrible day. Neighbors, friends, even strangers who would've perished if he hadn't acted so quickly.

He gave them a new life, inside a yam, which grew unexpectedly fast—this was true. But the giant potato provided shelter, food, and safety from the global disaster that was going on all around them.

The first ever Ejection was for Mr. Yamhill. Though it was not thought of as an Ejection, or even spoken of that way. It was a final release.

But happy news soon followed the creator's death.

Within two months of Mr. Yamhill's passing, a new child was born. During the next five years, more than a dozen children were born. Then double, even triple that number. And due to a now mono-flavored diet, with pregnant women getting their nutrients only from a feast of yams, skin color began to change.

Over the next ten, twenty, fifty years, all humans were tinted orange.

Xenophobia and racism were now forgotten things. Those types of ideas were created by the people of Old Earth, all of which had perished.

Hunger was no longer an issue.

Shelter was no longer an issue.

Providing a safe environment for your family was no longer an issue. Now the only issue was the lack of variety—in all things.

All people were a united People of the Potato.

And yet in all cultures, those of the Old Earth along with the new culture created by the survivors who now lived inside the protective barrier of Yam Hill, one thing could never be fully eradicated.

Men seeking power had not changed.

50

The idea of incarceration was disqualified immediately by the original group of survivors. This decision was based simply on the obvious fact that the prisoner, or prisoners, could simply use their hands to dig their way out—even eat their way to freedom. Prisoners would have to be watched constantly. And nobody wanted to volunteer for that job.

This was how the idea of Ejection was born.

This was also around the time when the idea of electing a group of men to rule over the growing population of Yam Hill took effect. The term Leaders quickly changed to Elders, and the rest is potato history.

Back then, there were Seven Elders, not three. Over the years, the number of Elders dwindled from seven, then five, then finally settling on no more than Three Elders at any given time. The less people who knew the truth, the better.

During the days of Old Earth, a book was once written declaring that 'the truth shall set you free.'

Then everyone died.

And now, during the days of Yam Hill, many years after the death of the Old Earth and everyone on it, there is a much more accurate statement.

The truth shall get you Ejected.

51

Minutes and hours are something that all residents of Yam Hill pay very little attention to. They are not important, and rarely counted, mainly because they could not be calculated by any accurate means.

A phrase such as "twenty minutes" could be closer to an hour. Much in the same way that an hour could feel like only twenty minutes had passed.

The Day Keeper did his best to keep a written potato log concerning the days, weeks, months, and years. As for keeping track of the minutes and hours, or getting somewhere on time, or the act of being late, those all belonged to Old Earth.

Roughly one minute had passed since Polly was Ejected. She had been released, back to Old Earth, where nothing survives.

52

Bic's Ejection would've gone faster if not for his lengthy protest. He defended himself rather well, and proved to the First Elder just how articulate a young man he had grown up to be. They had a good discussion.

But rules were rules, the Elder told him.

And the rules had been broken.

The first ever Double Ejection was over in less than two minutes.

Afterwards, the First Elder and Amadeus walked back down the steps, with the First Elder leading the way. No words were spoken until they reached their cordoned off living area, where great secrets were kept.

The deed was done, and work resumed.

Life on Yam Hill would carry on much like it had for these many, many years. Though not common knowledge, there is typically at least one rebellion during each potato generation.

Some of these rebellions were solo efforts, while others included up to a dozen (or more) angry or unsatisfied potato residents who wanted to question authority.

Sometimes a rebellion may involve just two young people, inspired to take action by an older resident, who was not only a well-respected Digger, but also an employee of the Elders.

People will always have an opinion.

People will always have a voice.

Those voices must sometimes be silenced. Stamped out, eradicated quickly, so that life inside the potato can carry on, as always, with plenty to eat and not much to accomplish. Such is the way of life, the new life.

Life in Yam Hill.

Old Earth

53

After tumbling more than two hundred feet, Bic finally came to a stop in a massive collection of fallen tree branches and shrubs. It was too dark to see that this pile must've been strategically placed here.

The majority of falling was done at a roughly forty-five-degree angle. Steeper in some areas, while more gradual in others. Several spots had nearly vertical drops, all mercifully ten feet or less. Bic somehow managed to tumble over every single one of them while Polly missed these sharp drops altogether.

If their long tumble had happened on a proper mountain, made of rock, the fall would've resulted in a broken arm, or leg, or possibly much worse—a broken neck, or broken back. The outer shell of Yam Hill was surprisingly soft.

Polly kept going.

She tumbled at least an extra hundred feet down the side of Yam Hill, well past Bic, sliding mostly on her back, or sides, or sometimes her face. But her long fall finally came to an end when she slammed up against a small, soft hill.

Nothing was broken, as far as she could tell. And the cuts and scrapes and bruises and gashes she received along the way would heal in time.

Most importantly, she was alive. Recently Ejected from Yam Hill, forcefully shoved out a small cutout in the side of the mountain-sized potato, tossed from the only home she'd ever known, back into a world that was uninhabitable and deadly. But she was still breathing, though even doing that hurt.

Not until a few hours later, when the great light from the sky appeared, would they get their first look around Old Earth. This was possible only because of the brilliant light provided by "the sun," which Polly and Bic had only read about in old books and seen in old magazines.

By its light, they discovered all the dead bodies.

54

The world was dark and full of shadows. To Polly and Bic, it appeared as though nothing had changed. Having grown up inside a giant yam, where every day is dark—or at least dim—this was the same as being inside Yam Hill, with barely enough light to see by.

Night and day had no meaning inside Yam Hill.

Taking a long look around, trying to process all that had happened, Polly wondered if this was all real.

"Maybe I'm still inside Yam Hill?" Polly thought. "Or maybe I'm dead?"

Bic screamed for help.

Polly ran to find him.

55

When a part of your body was bothering you, it was removed it. Depending on its size, or what it was, the person in pain typically decided if the body part would be removed or not. If the pain it caused was manageable during day-to-day potato life, it remained. If the pain it caused was bordering on unbearable, interfering with the continuation of a calm, sedentary potato life, steps had to be taken.

Pain was dealt with accordingly.

The handful of part-time Healers who worked inside Yam Hill were not doctors. These specially selected few— all men—were merely granted special permission from the Three Elders to borrow and read through the few medical books that were still inside the protected walls of their beloved yam. These were not complete books about medicine, but mostly magazines that described some basic procedures, along with some very complicated ones. There were usually pictures to go along with the procedures, plus more images of medical inventions from Old Earth, which no one inside Yam Hill had ever seen, or fully understood.

The medical magazines were only guidelines. None of them helped in any sort of way with any dental procedures, such as a painful tooth, the most common form of pain inside Yam Hill.

During the days of Old Earth, back before anesthesia was available, people who underwent any kind of surgical procedure would bite down hard on a "stick," a small section from a tree. Neither of which people from Yam Hill had ever seen, or touched.

Polly and Bic were the first ones from Yam Hill to witness, in real life, an Old Earth tree. There were hundreds of them, perhaps thousands, all around them. Too many to see properly in the dark.

And it was a small piece of one of these trees, a small length of branch that, during their long fall, had forced its way inside Bic's body. Thankfully, it had missed any vital organs, but did manage to puncture him just above the left hip bone. The stick, flat on one end and very sharp on the other, had lodged itself approximately four inches into Bic's side.

He didn't notice the pain until he tried to sit up.

56

The red glow of LEDs inside Yam Hill is an everyday occurrence.

The sight of blood is extremely rare.

57

"Bic!" Polly shouted. "Where are you?"

When he didn't answer, Polly nearly broke down. If she stuck wandering around Old Earth, in the dark, all alone, she didn't want to live anymore.

"I'm here!" Bic finally said. "Are you okay?"

"Yes, I'm okay," Polly hollered back, still trying to locate her friend. As she rushed back up Yam Hill, trying to locate him, she tripped on anything and everything along the way.

"Keep talking so I can find you!" Polly shouted.

Bic kept talking.

Polly aimed in the direction of his voice. The climb was all uphill, but never too steep. The terrain under her feet was familiar potato skin.

At first, Polly didn't realize she was naked. Too much had happened in the last few minutes to realize that, at some point during the fall, her potato skin covering had come completely off her body. She would have to find it after she was reunited with Bic. Right now, it was much too dark, and Bic was screaming at her about something.

"POLLY!" Bic shouted. "There's something stuck in me! It's inside me! Get it out! It hurts!"

Polly was thankful beyond words to hear the voice of her friend, even though he was screaming about the severe pain he was currently experiencing. She was thankful to not be alone out here, wherever here actually was.

"Bic, keep talking!" Polly said. "I have no idea where you are!"

"I'm leaking!" Bic's voice was strained, near panic. He didn't know how to describe the object that was jutting out of his left side. It hurt when he moved. It hurt when he didn't move.

"I think it's blood, Polly. I'm not sure. It's too dark to tell."

"How bad?" Polly asked, getting closer.

"I don't know! Just hurry up," Bic hollered back. "There's a...there's a thing sticking in me!"

Polly nearly tripped over him in the dark. "Found you."

"Finally," Bic said. "Polly, what took you so long? I kept talking like you said. And I..." Bic trailed off. His eyes grew very large, and his pain was momentarily forgotten.

Even in the darkness, especially up close, the naked human form can easily be distinguished from one that is fully clothed.

Temperature never wavered inside Yam Hill, so her body's reaction to the cool night air was completely foreign.

"Polly? But you're..." Bic's brain was suddenly unable to think of words or form sentences used for speaking. Aside from seeing himself naked, he had never once in all his life seen another person without their potato skin covering.

"You're naked, Polly." Bic stated this as if his friend was unaware of her outwardly appearance.

"Stop staring at me, Bic." Polly forced herself to not be embarrassed. And she really had no reason to be. It was dark, but not quite dark enough to completely veil her body.

"Sorry," Bic said, trying not to stare, though he could've tried harder. She was so close to him, so near to his own body that it was nearly impossible not to look.

Bic couldn't find the right words. Finally, he settled on: "Polly, you're beautiful."

"Thank you, Bic," Polly said in a tone that suggested he better change the subject. "But right now, I am trying to get this sharp thing, whatever it is, out of your body. Be still. Don't move."

Trying to distract him, she told the story about how she once got to see her mother remove a lady's tooth.

"My mother used an Elder-approved book," Polly explained. "Not for reading, but so the lady could bite down on something hard. Then she pulled the tooth out with her fingers Now hold still, will you? I'm just going to…"

"Going to what?" Bic began to pull away from her.

"Okay, you can look at me," Polly said, "but only for a few seconds."

"AHH!"

Bic did look. And that was precisely the moment when Polly pulled the painful object out of his side. The stick was removed, then thrown away into the surrounding darkness, as if it were still dangerous.

"You okay?" Polly asked.

"No," Bic said. "That hurt—a lot. I'd rather be Ejected again than have one of those things stuck inside me."

With the palm of her hand, Polly felt around for a smooth patch. She struggled a bit at first, but managed to peel back a small section of potato skin. Then she shoved her hand down inside and scooped up a small handful of fresh yam. She used both hands to mash it into a workable paste. Then, with plenty of grimacing from Bic, and plenty of complaining about how cold it was, she placed the remedy on her friend's wound.

"That's the best I can do right now," Polly said. "I don't know if I fixed you or not. But at least that thing isn't stuck inside you anymore." Gently, she put one hand to his cheek. Then, not so gently, she pushed him away so he would stop looking at her.

"Bic?"

"Sorry," Bic said. "I was staring again, wasn't I?"

Although he'd been around her practically every day of his life, seeing her like this was different. Vastly different. He knew he had to stop staring or else face Polly's anger. There was only one way he could think of to put up a barrier between his curious eyes and Polly's skin.

"Wait right here." Bic carefully stood up, clearly overacting about how much pain he was experiencing. Then he began to search around the immediate area to find something that Polly could use to at least partially cover herself up.

Bic knelt down and dug his hands into the outer potato skin, then pulled. The first section he pulled up sent him backwards, surprising him when the piece suddenly came free.

"Are you okay?" Polly asked.

"Yes, I'm fine," Bic answered. "I'm just working on something. Might take me a little while, though."

"What are you doing?"

"I'm trying to make you something." Bic pulled as hard as he could, managing to get a good start on a new section. "I'm trying to make you a new body covering. This isn't as easy as I always assumed it was. Diggers really do work hard. I need some more time for this. Just sit where you are, Polly. Don't go anywhere. I don't want to lose you again."

Polly assured him that she wasn't going to move. She was too exhausted, too sore to move. Her muscles ached, her back and neck hurt, even her mind ached. All she wanted to do was close her eyes. Sleep. Dream that her life and everything she knew hadn't been Ejected.

Although it took some time, more than twenty minutes, which was just enough time for Polly to fall into a light sleep, Bic finally managed to tear away a section of potato skin that would work.

What he held up was similar to the potato skin blankets they both had back inside their potato homes. This one wasn't trimmed, or softened, but it should work for one night.

Thinking about his own potato bed, his own potato skin blanket, and all the comforts of his old home, was too much to bear right now. Polly and Bic were now both without a home.

"GET AWAY!"

Bic jumped back. "Polly, it's me. It's okay."

"Where is—?" Polly was on high alert, ready to fight. "Sorry, Bic. I thought..." Having somehow fallen asleep in an awkward position, with her knees propped up and head resting on her arms, she was startled awake when something large and heavy slipped over her shoulders and back.

"Thank you," Polly said, wrapping herself up in her new potato skin blanket. It was much rougher than her old one, but she was thankful to have it.

"You scared me," said Bic. He sat down bedside her, but not too close. He'd already upset Polly by staring at her uncovered body, so hoped he made up for it by providing her some privacy.

"Sorry for shouting at you like that," Polly said. "I think I fell asleep. I thought you were the First Elder, or someone trying to grab me."

Images of the First Elder pulling and dragging her along while informing her how much it pained *him* that she had to be Ejected "...for the sake of Yam Hill..." and all sorts of other lies, suddenly flooded back. Out here there were no Elders. No one to harm them. Not even any sounds. Only them.

"I can still feel his hands on me," Polly said, unable to push the recent memory away. "Pulling me, and hurting me. His breath was terrible too. And I think he ripped out some of my hair. That might've been an accident, though, after I kicked him as hard as I could."

Bic remembered it all too well. Although he was a good distance behind Polly, he could certainly hear his best friend screaming at the First Elder, yelling at him to let her go. Sometimes he overheard her talking to him, trying to reason with him as he dragged her along, through hallway after hallway, up and down potato stairwells, begging him to release her.

Bic and Amadeus, the wild-eyed hairy man with hardly any teeth, did their best to keep up with the fast-moving First Elder. Amadeus, the eager new employee of the Three Elders, was not a nice man. He kept saying awful things to Bic, and shoving him from behind. He used the Old Earth rifle to prod him along, jabbing it into Bic's lower and upper back. And more than once, he smacked it into the back of Bic's skull, then laughed at the pain it caused.

Bic cringed every time the Old Earth rifle touched him. One reason was because of the pain, but the main reason was that he didn't want the gun to explode again, to hear that awful noise it made, so painfully loud.

Polly took the worst of it. She was tough, but now she seemed deflated. Sad. Defeated.

"I'm sorry all that happened to you, Polly," Bic said. "The First Elder had no right to do that. Any of it. And I thought—" Bic looked away, thinking. "I always thought they were supposed to protect us. I was raised to believe the Three Elders are great men, better than everyone else. My parents taught me that we should love the Elders, always."

Polly fell silent.

After a long time, Bic said: "Those were some excellent kicks, Polly. I think you actually hurt the First Elder. You're the only one I know who has actually kicked another person. I wish I could've seen it up close. When me and that Amadeus man hurried and caught up to you two, I saw you fighting against him in the hallway. You were really brave."

Polly looked down. "Brave enough to get us both Ejected."

Bic could tell that she was already blaming herself for what happened. It probably didn't help matters with Polly cursing at the First Elder, kicking him, scratching and biting him, but it was clear they were going to be Ejected, no matter what they said or did.

"At least we're not alone," Bic said. "We're together, Polly. I'd hate to be out here by myself." He looked around, trying to see in the dark, wondering what life would be like in constant darkness.

Polly inched closer to Bic. She pulled her new potato skin blanket tight around her, shivering.

"I just hope the outside world doesn't get any darker," Bic said. "This isn't at all what I expected. I don't really know what I expected, but not this. I thought the outside world would be loud and horrible. This place doesn't even have—"

Bic stopped.

After looking up, way up, straining his neck, Bic found that he could no longer talk. His words had all dried up. His mind went blank.

The entire world above their heads had opened up to reveal bright specks of light.

"Doesn't what?" Polly said. "What's wrong?"

"LOOK!"

Polly nearly jumped out of her potato skin blanket when Bic grabbed her roughly by the back of the neck. She was sick of shouting, sick of being startled, sick of uninvited hands on her body. But as soon as she looked up, all those worries were immediately forgotten. She too became completely entranced by what was up there. And how many of them there were.

Stars.

"Look at them all, Polly!" Bic was beyond excited. "Those are stars, real ones! Just like in all those Elder-approved magazines. They do exist."

Tiny bright dots lit up the nighttime sky. They were beyond counting, although Bic did try to tally them up, then quit soon after.

Polly had also read about stars, though it was probably years ago, picking up an Old Earth magazine after her mother and father had finished reading it.

"They're amazing," Polly said, equally impressed.

The two of them lay back together, stretching out at an angle, with their heads pointed up Yam Hill, in the direction of the Ejection site.

Words, at least words they knew, could not begin to describe what they were seeing. A picture of the star-filled night sky on the pages of a faded magazine could not accurately show how incredible the sight truly was. Some stars looked close enough that she could reach out and touch them.

Neither one of them had any clue how long they stayed up, staring at the stars. An hour or two, probably longer.

At some point, Polly yawned.

The night air was cool, but not cold enough that either of them would freeze overnight. Falling asleep was not a huge worry. Polly and Bic were lying side by side. They were now so close that Polly could feel Bic's weight pressed against her. She thought about inviting Bic to sleep underneath the potato skin blanket with her, but not when she had no potato covering on.

Appropriate behavior was important inside Yam Hill—extremely important. And even though they were Ejected, no longer considered residents of Yam Hill, appropriate behavior was still important, even if it was to be their last night alive.

Perhaps they would fall asleep, one last time, and simply not wake up. The outside world, Old Earth, was nothing like Yam Hill.

Polly imagined that maybe she might wake up inside her dreams. Better than living in the continual darkness of Old Earth, even if there were amazing stars to look up at.

Not waking up might not be so bad.

While dozing off, Polly forced all the dark thoughts from her mind. Maybe after a rest, then waking up with a fresh mind, they wouldn't feel so helpless. So lost and alone.

In the dark, Polly pulled her right arm out from underneath her potato skin blanket. She reached out and grabbed hold of Bic's hand. At least they had each other to rely on while trapped in this dark new world.

Lying at an angle underneath the stars and clouds, instead of in their soft yam beds, with their scratchy but warm potato skin blankets, both of them were able to fall asleep within a matter of minutes.

58

There were no dreams.

After what felt like only minutes, but was more than five hours of uninterrupted sleep, Polly felt her mind slowly swirling back to consciousness.

Bic was not beside her.

Polly didn't hear her best friend snap awake. Not even when he cried out in his sleep. Bic had come out of a dead sleep, panicked, as if something was terribly wrong. His tired mind had also remained dreamless, but he thought that maybe he'd heard a noise. Something out there, in the dark, approaching quickly, possibly searching them out.

That was more than two hours ago.

Polly still didn't wake up when Bic pulled away from her, almost in a clumsy effort. He accidently bumped her, twice, and still she never stirred in her sleep. She slept right through the night, as Bic walked off to search for her potato skin covering, with tree branches and twigs cracking and crunching under his feet.

When he left their potato site, the stars above still provided some light, which was helpful. But the greatest improvement was how the sky had taken on a lighter shade of darkness. And it continued to grow even lighter. This drastic change was happening everywhere, stretching out as far as he could see.

Bic stared at the proceedings with an intensely worried look on his face. Something was happening to Old Earth, and he had to warn Polly. But soon his worried face turned to a more thoughtful, curious expression when he finally realized what was going on.

The event caused pain in his eyes, it was so bright.

After a lifetime of only being able to read about this particular event in old books and magazines, Bic was the first person to witness this spectacular event.

A sunrise.

59

The great thinkers of Old Earth made many great discoveries prior to the Great Unexpected Tragedy. Wonderful things were uncovered, then revealed to a most curious world. Mysteries were uncovered and opened up for all people to see and understand.

One discovery was how the sun, which was used by all people and all living creatures of Old Earth, was strategically placed way up high in the upper atmosphere. Far enough away that its incredible heat didn't incinerate everyone, but close enough so that it did not allow everyone to freeze to death.

Every day, people learned more.

But all that learning, all those great discoveries, all those mysteries and secrets they uncovered, still could not protect them. Their knowledge didn't save them.

The Great Unexpected Tragedy surprised even the smartest and most recognized scientists and professors of Old Earth.

By then, it was too late.

All people, including those with the highest degrees of education, were bound to the Earth by gravity. And when it failed, nobody knew how to fix it.

They too screamed for their lives.

All the way up into the atmosphere.

60

Most people of Old Earth believed that all the human race needed to survive was food, water, and air. Gravity was always taken for granted.

61

Even after so many years, after the massive time gap that the Three Elders always reminded people separated their generation from the Old Earth's final generation, looking directly at the still sun still hurts your eyes.

Bic found this out after only a few minutes.

The sun had lost none of its power or its magnificence. The brilliant shining star still possessed the ability to quickly cause the cornea layer to blister and crack, or even permanently damage the retina with its powerful UV light. This type of severe harm only happened if a person stared directly into the sun for an extended period. Which was exactly what Bic was doing, right up until he yelled out loud, then finally looked away. Wisely, he then held one hand up to shield the great light from causing any further damage.

"Incredible." Bic was standing somewhere in the middle of a giant yam, experiencing the first sunrise seen by a resident (ex-resident) of Yam Hill, after so many years of living in the dark.

This was absolutely the greatest experience of his young life. He wanted to wake up Polly, so she could share this amazing moment with him. But she looked so peaceful as she slept, all curled up underneath her new potato skin blanket.

With near-perfect timing, right as Bic looked at her with great affection, a natural affinity, even love, and a peaceful quiet for miles in every direction, Polly let out a great loud snore and nearly woke herself up.

Bic laughed.

Polly's own sleeping noises practically startled her awake. She lay underneath her thick potato skin blanket, eyes closed, not quite ready to face another day. Yesterday was rough: three Ejections, one of which was her own.

What Bic had read, in several Elder-approved books and magazines, was that sunlight lasted for a large part of each day. So she too would have time to enjoy its light.

The sun was completely visible within a few minutes, exposing everything, illuminating their pale, undernourished, orange-tinted bodies with warm light.

Instead of enjoying the sight, Polly screamed.

"BIC! Help me!" Polly cried out, pleading with him to turn off a "light" he had no control over.

Bic had no idea that Polly would be this scared. At first, he thought she was joking, so laughed it off. But she truly was frightened. Polly was certain her skin, possibly her whole body would melt away.

"Bic! What's happening?" Polly finally opened her eyes, but only enough to take a quick look around. Then she quickly sat up and put her hands to her face, attempting to block out the sunlight and keep it from causing any more harm.

"Calm yourself," Bic said, coming closer. "Relax. It's perfectly okay. Nothing is going to hurt you."

"Make it stop!" Polly threw an arm over her head, as if that would fend off the unyielding light. The strange new light was so bright it hurt her eyes.

"Polly, you'll be okay. Trust me." Bic knelt down beside her. "The light isn't going to hurt us. It's the sun, Polly. The sun."

Polly opened her eyes, only a little. "What are you talking about? You mean—from books?"

"No, Polly, I mean it's the sun. The real sun." Bic was smiling and happy, not being burned up. "The same sun we've read about since we were little. It's real, too!"

"I can see that, Bic," Polly said, and held up her blanket like a shield. She still refused to fully open her eyes. Too painful. "Well, I can almost see it. How can so much light make it hard to see?"

"Don't worry," Bic told her. "Your eyes will become used to it, eventually. Just don't stare at it for too long. I did. Now I've got these little dancing, blinking lights stuck on my eyes."

Bic informed her that he found something else. He hoped his discovery would stop her from being so frightened. She was trembling, he saw, all over her beautiful skin. Her shoulders, fully exposed, were pulled tight in a defensive posture.

"I found your covering," Bic told her.

Polly's front was covered, clinging tight to her potato skin blanket, but most of her back was fully exposed in the light.

"You did?" Polly immediately forgot about the sunrise, an epic event that had not been witnessed by anyone since the Great Unexpected Tragedy.

Bic found it amusing that Polly seemed happier that he'd found her old covering, much preferring that over the spectacular sunrise.

"How did you find it?" Polly asked.

"I've been awake for a long time," Bic told her. "Something woke me up. A noise, I guess."

"What noise?" Polly asked. "There's no one out here but us. Right?"

"I don't think it was anything," Bic said, even though he was positive that he did hear something. The sound of a faraway voice, maybe even shouting.

Bic held up her potato skin covering.

Polly stood up without the blanket.

Bic had known Polly for most of his life. If she had wanted him not to see, she would've said something, told him to turn around, or asked him to look away. Knowing Polly, she probably would've hit him if he dared to look when he shouldn't have.

Bic was still in awe of how beautiful she was.

"Thank you, Bic!"

"Of course. You're my best friend."

Polly got dressed, loving the feeling of her own personal potato skin covering. Having it on seemed to make things a bit less stressful, or at least more tolerable.

Polly noticed the way Bic was smiling at her. "What's wrong?"

"I found something else," Bic told her.

"You did?" Polly asked. "What is it? A way back inside?"

Bic shook his head. "No, I didn't find a way back inside. What I did find, I think you'll like it. I didn't know what it was at first. When I walked up the hill, just over there—" He pointed back up the jagged hill. "I thought it was just another part of Yam Hill. But then I looked closer and saw the writing inside."

Polly hated it when he didn't come right out and say things. But this time, she couldn't have been happier. She was certain he had found what she had worked so hard to protect, but could no longer hold on to while tumbling down the side of Yam Hill.

Bic smiled.

"You really found it?" Polly asked.

From behind his back, Bic produced a long, rolled up length of potato skin. He was happy to see how pleased she was by his discovery.

"Is that it?" Polly asked, staring at it for a moment. "I can't believe you found it!"

What she had tried so hard to keep hidden from the First Elder, all while he dragged her through Yam Hill, was in their possession once more.

Out here in the daylight, the potato skin scroll looked much smaller than it did back in the red glow of Jack of Heart's room. But here it was, still in one piece, and still legible.

Last night, Polly had cried herself to sleep over losing it. Now it seems they were wasted tears.

Bic found Jack of Hearts' letter.

62

Communication by use of pictures and drawings outdates the written word. Back in the early days of Old Earth—the very early days, when trading goods with people in faraway lands began to increase—the idea of writing letters was created.

Jack of Hearts' letter had both words and pictures.

Polly had no idea Jack of Hearts was so creative. Aside from being a well-respected, hard-working Digger, he was also a talented artist. If she had known this back when he was alive, she would've loved to have sat down with him and carved out a potato skin picture together, or created some kind of yam sculpture. It could've been something of his to keep in her room, so she could enjoy it while he was away working, or on special assignments for the Elders.

That opportunity had been stolen.

Jack of Hearts had been taken from her, ripped from her life. All future conversations, shared laughs, and any quality time together had been stolen by the Three

Elders, the very people that all residents of Yam Hill are supposed to trust above all others.

63

As they were leaving Jack of Hearts' room, thinking they were headed home after a traumatic experience—witnessing, or at least listening to an illegal Ejection—Polly's foot had kicked against something soft.

The letter.

Polly had managed to find it in the dark, nearly tripping over it. While still managing to hold Bic's hand, she was able to quickly bend down, scoop it up, then slip it underneath her potato skin covering, all without missing a step.

When they headed out into the hallway a moment later, as she was still trying to maneuver the thick letter into a more comfortable position, they stepped into the hallway and ran right into the First Elder and Amadeus.

Polly worked hard to keep the letter concealed. It was hers, and she intended to keep it hidden.

Focusing on that helped her to deal with the pain of being dragged through the hallways, up and down staircases, being lead to her death by a man who easily overpowered her.

With all the dragging and pulling going on at the hands of the surprisingly strong First Elder, Polly did her best to break free. If she hadn't desperately been trying to keep the letter hidden underneath her potato skin covering, she might have been able to break free.

But then what? She would've had to spend the rest of her life in hiding, alone, always changing locations, living in constant fear. That type of life would be unbearable, trying to remain unseen, even amongst so many residents who preferred to live the smallest life imaginable.

Instead, she clung to the letter. It was her safety, her life, her future inside Yam Hill that she couldn't hold on to.

Polly was Ejected while still clinging to Jack of Heart's potato skin letter.

64

"I sort of…" Bic looked embarrassed.

"What?" Polly asked. "You're not hurt again, are you? If I have to pull another one of those tree branches out of your side, I think I'll make you do it. I tried to be tough, but that was really awful. Blood was leaking out of you."

"No, I'm fine," Bic said, then gently touched his hurt side. "But your letter—it might've gotten ripped. But only a little bit. Somewhere in the middle, I think. I rolled it back up carefully as I could, I promise."

Polly didn't care. She was simply thrilled to have it, rip or no rip. The last remaining evidence of her late friend, Jack of Hearts, was safe in her arms. And she would not lose it again. Maybe it contained some clues, or ideas for their survival upon Old Earth.

"Let's read it!" Polly kneeled down and excitedly began to unravel the scroll. Before she managed to unroll it even a few feet, Bic's hand was on her shoulder.

From her knees, Polly looked up. "What's wrong?"

Bic said nothing, only pointed.

When Polly stood up, the dizziness from that simple action nearly caused her to fall back down again. She'd eaten nothing since long before their Ejection. Still, she managed to stay upright despite the rapid drop in blood pressure.

Judging by the bits of yam on Bic's potato skin covering, he'd already eaten some breakfast. Polly would have to do the same if she was to have any energy to get through this most unusual day. The menu was the same as it was inside: yams for breakfast, lunch, and dinner.

"We can read the letter somewhere else, Polly," Bic said. "But not here. I've been trying to not look over there all morning."

Polly stared at the familiar shapes for a long time. Even with the incredible light from the sun, it still didn't register. Her mind refused to believe what it was actually seeing.

Potato coverings.

Bodies.

A large pile of Ejected people.

"Are those—? It can't be." Polly guessed the large pile of body coverings was eight to ten feet high.

"Those are body coverings, Bic," Polly said, perhaps saying the words out loud for her own marginal comfort. "Not the kind that we wear. Those look like the kind or coverings that people are wrapped in before they're Ejected."

"Yes, I know, Polly." Bic had most of the morning to process this new gruesome discovery. "I think Jack of Hearts was right. There's a lot of things we don't understand about Yam Hill."

Some bodies had been lying there so long that trees were growing on top of the potato skins. Some of the wrapped bodies appeared to be half-buried, as if partially swallowed, returning to Yam Hill.

Others looked relatively new.

"Polly, where are you going?" Bic didn't move from his spot. He would go no further. If Polly wanted to take a closer look, that would be her choice.

Polly knelt down to read the inscription.

Hallelujah Geyser

"Polly? What are you doing?" Bic didn't like what she was about to do, but he wasn't going to rush over and stop her. If anything, he wanted to back away further.

"I just want to make sure it's him," Polly said as she kneeled down. She reached out her hand, about to peel back the cover.

"Don't do it, Polly." Bic pleaded with her, but she refused to listen.

"Just wait," Polly said. "I'll prove it's not him."

"I saw his name carved into the potato skin covering," Bic told her, hopefully in a harsh enough tone that it would deter her from doing what she was about to do. "It's him, Polly. Trust me."

"Yes, I can see the name carved into the potato skin, too," Polly said, "but I want to make sure. Maybe these aren't bodies at all, Bic. Did you ever think of that? Maybe they're the coverings that were never used. Old pieces of potato skin that were—"

Polly stood up, quickly. Back straight, arms at her side, practically frozen.

"What?" Bic said, alarmed. "What is it?"

Polly shook it off and rushed back to where Bic was standing, then hid behind him. Her hands, her whole body was shaking as she hung on tight to Bic's potato skin covering.

"It's him," Polly said, peeking at pile of bodies from behind her friend. "I saw a hand in there. And his arm, I think. There's a body in there, Bic. A *real* body. I thought Ejected people were all supposed to go somewhere. You know, up. Somewhere away from Yam Hill."

The Three Elders had always said that when a person is Ejected, the body travels up, very high, further than anyone can see. What happened next, even the Elders didn't know. Bic always thought of it as a burial in the sky, floating upwards in a brilliant release, then turning into nothing—blackness, no different than an LED that stopped working.

Every resident of Yam Hill thought roughly the same thing. Only because this is what the Three Elders had told them.

The truth was piled high. And in plain view.

"Do you believe me now?" Although Bic enjoyed having Polly this close, standing behind him, feeling her warm breath come and go on the side of his neck, he wished to be far, far away from this disposal site.

Polly did not speak, only nodded.

"Good," Bic said. "Can we leave now?"

Polly agreed by nodding, yes, over and over. She practically dragged Bic by the shoulder of his potato skin covering, pulling him along so they could get away as fast as possible. Far away from the pile of Ejected bodies, which were supposed to be in some other world, not in a pile at the bottom of the Ejection site.

More Elder lies.

The two of them did not walk away from the pile of bodies, or walk as fast as they possibly could on the rough, potato skin terrain.

They ran.

65

Running inside Yam Hill was done on soft, well-travelled yam, spongy underneath the traveler's feet. Running on hard potato skin hurt.

66

During all her visits to Mr. Geyser's Clothes Maker shop—and to Mrs. Geyser's Clothes Maker shop, in the next hallway over—Polly had always enjoyed speaking with Mr. Geyser better. Not that Mrs. Geyser wasn't fun to visit. It was merely that she seemed the saddest of the two. Sad not only because she and her husband could not have children naturally, but they were also denied reception (*adoption*, using in Old Earth terminology) by the Three Elders.

Mrs. Geyser echoed sadness.

Polly could always sense it during her visits to Mrs. Geyser's shop. The subject of "children" always came up quickly in conversation. Then the sadness would come out. It was In her face, in her eyes—especially her eyes. Polly would usually (not always, but usually) allow Mrs. Geyser's request to come closer, even ask for a full body embrace. Mrs. Geyser would come out from behind her potato work bench, sit close to Polly, and just look at her. Stare at her, and smile. Her eyes would fill up, and Polly knew that the tears would soon follow.

"I see so much of me in you, Polly," Mrs. Geyser would say, or something similar. Then she would gently touch Polly's face, staring into it with her watery orange eyes. That's when Polly would make up an excuse, anything, so she could leave. She would usually say that Bic was waiting on her.

Being purposely kept in the dark—not merely in the dim LED light of Yam Hill, but in all things—Polly had no idea of knowing that Evermore Geyser, known as Mrs. Geyser to all her customers, had been born to the same mother as Polly, many years before.

Sisters, but from different fathers.

67

Jack of Hearts visited the Geyser's often. Being the boss of the largest Digging Crew inside Yam Hill, he would delegate one of his subordinates to drop off the freshly cut potato skins to all the Clothes Maker's shops.

But Jack of Hearts personally delivered the fresh potato skins to Mr. and Mrs. Geyser, usually on his way home. Potato skins that he had personally carved from the outer edges of Yam Hill, carrying as many as he could manage, or dragging extras, if requested, on another piece of potato skin that could be pulled along behind him.

Only because of Jack of Hearts' strong friendship with the Geyser's did Polly know that Mr. Geyser's first name was Hallelujah, an Old Earth word that had something to do with becoming a "spirit," the very thing that Elders always said happens to a body after it is Ejected.

Not lying in a heap outside of Yam Hill.

68

Leaving the burial site could've gone one of two ways. If they had looked more carefully, towards the south side of the Ejected bodies, they've would've seen a path. This path, though grown over in small sections, had been cleared by someone who had visited this site many times, trying to place the bodies in a more respectable manner. The path led right to the bottom of Yam Hill, straight down to the flatlands of Old Earth.

Polly and Bic fled in the opposite direction.

Being in a hurry, and certainly not wishing to get any closer to the pile of Ejected people, Polly and Bic opted for the simpler route, which led them past numerous other potato skin-wrapped bodies.

Ejected people, scattered everywhere.

Because of the terrain, both of them ended up being forced to step over numerous bodies. Ejected residents that had travelled down the side of Yam Hill much further than all the others—some fifty, a hundred, even two hundred feet further, or more. One of the last bodies required them to work together to get around it, to squeeze through a narrow section between two potato walls.

Polly didn't want to see the words, but saw them regardless. Bic also read the name attached.

Evermore Geyser

69

The Ejection process is performed in a truly respectful manner. Though the final act is quite crude, with one of the Elders literally shoving the wrapped body out of a square cutout in the side of Yam Hill, everything up to that point is done with absolute care.

If the one who has died was well-respected, lived a non-disruptive life, or was simply a valued resident, the Three Elders saw to it that every detail was meticulously carried out. They made sure the deceased was properly stored and treated with great care.

Several high-quality potato skins were selected, always carved out new, then a very long, very thin strand of potato skin was chosen for wrapping. The body would be tied in a very specific way, so that the Ejected body would remain securely wrapped for the rest of their journey.

Sometimes, though not very often, one of the Elders oversaw the entire process. This usually only happened if there was some biological relation to the deceased.

Others were treated quite differently.

Residents who were not well-respected, such as Solitaires, were Ejected as quickly as possible, without alerting anyone. The deceased would be rolled up in a basic potato skin covering—same as rolling a carpet in the days of Old Earth—and then unceremoniously discarded from Yam Hill.

Sometimes the final potato skin coverings of the Solitaires stayed together better than the bodies that were given top honors. Those bodies that were wrapped up meticulously and with great care, but managed to spill open shortly after Ejection.

Everything eventually returned to Yam Hill.

In some way.

70

During the first hour, Polly and Bic were able to travel relatively unobstructed. They made some real downward progress. Both were able to descend the side of Yam Hill at about the same speed as travelling inside the great potato.

Sharp drops, thick patches of trees, and large indentations in the outer skin soon began to inhibit their quick pace.

The two travelers scaled down the steep, nearly vertical walls and cliffs as best they could. Bic would lay on his stomach, arms stretched to the maximum, and then he would drop Polly as gently as he could, down to the next lower level. Then Bic would climb down after her, usually ending up dropping most of the distance.

Most times the landings were soft. But not always.

"Are you hurt?" Polly helped Bic sit up after a particularly bad landing. Bic landed fine, but went sailing backwards in the opposite direction that Polly had her arms out to catch him. He took a bad bounce and ended up twisting his ankle.

"Yes, I think so," Bic said, obviously lying. His face was red from strain and he was clutching his right ankle.

"Will you just sit down for a minute, please?" Polly shoved him back down after he immediately tried to stand up.

Bic wisely agreed to rest a moment.

After taking a few minutes to rest, with his back up against Yam Hill, gently stretching out his injured ankle, he felt he could go on. But now travel was slower than before.

Soon the sun was directly overhead. Neither of them had experienced this much heat, or sweat, or dehydration. The sun was immensely powerful. And it was wearing them down.

71

Bic enjoyed walking beside Polly most of all. Although he did manage to find her potato skin covering, he could not locate the tie-wrap. Residents used them to secure their coverings around the waist, to avoid any unwanted side exposure.

"Stop it," Polly said, again.

Bic tried to focus on his walking.

72

Walking up or down a set of well-maintained, smooth, carved potato steps is a relatively easy task, depending on the size of the staircase. Some stairwells inside Yam Hill are a dozen steps or less. Others can be hundreds of steps high. Several of the longer staircases, the ones that lead to the upper floors, approached the 1000-step mark.

The Ejection Site held the record: 2080 steps.

73

The act of "sweating" was not altogether common inside Yam Hill. Adults spent their days sitting and reading, eating and reading, sleeping and napping. Typically, most adults would venture outside their potato home 2-3 times a week, stepping into the hallway to speak with a friend, or perhaps to travel a short distance to visit with a neighbor.

Children who played games, or explored, or ran up and down the potato hallways and stairwells would often feel the sensation of sweat on their arms, back, or face. But even young children, sometimes as early as five or six years old, quit moving around so much. They adopted the same sedentary lifestyle as their parents.

Many residents of Yam Hill had lived their entire lives without once experiencing the act of sweating, and perhaps thought it to be a rumor.

During Polly's explorations, she would often work up enough body heat to perspire. Exploring, especially with Polly, could last for hours. But most of the exploring was done while walking, not running, and certainly not underneath a massive heat lamp in the sky.

Sweating under a hot sun, especially to someone new to the Old Earth and its unwelcoming environment, was not something that anyone from Yam Hill had ever experienced before. Polly couldn't imagine that even the long gone residents of Old Earth truly enjoyed the experience of immense heat, sweating, dehydration, and the toll it took on a body.

Polly was not enjoying herself. And she made this clear to Bic, her travelling partner, every chance she could. This was the reason, she assumed, that he was walking so far ahead of her. Her only option was to take off her potato skin covering and carry it with her. That would be inappropriate, so she was content to complain about the heat, at great length, as they wandered Old Earth, searching for a sign of...anything.

<h1 style="text-align:center">74</h1>

"You snored last night." Bic was trying to alleviate some of the uneasiness of their situation. Both of them were tired, hot, grumpy, recently Ejected from Yam Hill, and speaking to each other only in short sentences.

After a few dozen yards, Polly replied: "I do not snore, Bic."

Exploring adventures inside Yam Hill had always been fun. And if either of them had enough, or needed to go home, the adventure could be called off at any time, for any reason. But this adventure could not be called off. Not for any reason. They had to see it through until the end, no matter the outcome.

"Actually, you do," Bic said. "Really loud, too."

Polly decided it was too hot to argue.

Bic knew Polly well, much better than she gave him credit for. He could manipulate conversations and situations just as well as she could. After all, he'd learned it from her. If he kept quiet, she would eventually see that he was right, then relent and agree. It had worked many times in the past.

Bic continued to lead the way, in silence.

"I'll bet you snore," Polly said some time later. "Probably as loud as some Old Earth animal, I bet."

Despite the risk of being hit, or punched, or ignored, Bic said, "I don't know if I snore, but I promise that *you* snore. One was so loud, you woke yourself up. But you went right back to sleep."

Polly smiled, only a little. Bic couldn't see it because he was walking in front of her, trying to lead them down the least treacherous path.

There was no path.

Yam Hill was slanted in most spots, on top of being dangerously steep in other areas. Some routes, if they weren't paying attention, would lead them back up Yam Hill, in the complete opposite direction of what they were trying to achieve, which was to get to the bottom.

Their giant, beloved potato was anything but easy to descend. There were grooves, and cracks, and narrow walkways to travel along, but most were oddly-shaped, twisted, not straight at all, with hardly enough room for their feet.

"Does it bother you that I snored?" Polly asked.

Without hesitating, Bic said, "Yes." Then, turning around with a smile, he told her the truth.

"No, it doesn't bother me," Bic said. "My father snores every night."

Further down the mountainside, Bic had had no choice but to lead them through a large V-shaped opening that was particularly difficult to descend. This tight spot was nearly twenty feet tall, with potato walls on either side of them, and no way around it.

"My father snores too," Polly said. She had to carefully place each foot in front of the other, or risk twisting her ankle just like Bic had earlier. "Now that I think of it, so does my mother. I only know that because the only chance I ever had to read anything was at night, when I couldn't sleep. They'd be in their bedroom, sleeping another day away—"

"Snoring away, you mean."

"Exactly. I'll be in the main room, reading their books and magazines for a long time, and I'll hear them both snoring." Polly slipped once, but managed to keep her balance.

"Sometimes I read until I fall asleep," Polly went on. "Right there on the table."

Talking eased their fears. It allowed them both to not focus on their hopeless situation.

After nearly a thirty-minute struggle, Bic came out the other side of the incredibly long, and very claustrophobic section of Yam Hill. He was proud that he didn't injure his ankle further.

Immediately after he came out the other side, Yam Hill opened up to a wide, flat area, stretching out for at least a ten-minute walk in any direction. There were still a handful of trees not too far off, but this patch was comparably small. The rest of Yam Hill was absolutely covered with tall Old Earth trees.

Polly was still struggling.

"Need help?" Bic asked, reaching out a hand.

Polly was at least fifteen feet away, and still a good ten feet above where Bic was standing.

"No, I'm fine." Polly watched her feet, taking careful steps. "Just let me concentrate, okay?" One misstep and she would've crash-landed right on top of Bic.

"Okay," Bic said, and drew his hand back.

Sensing she might've hurt his feelings, Polly said, "I think if I tried to reach down right now—" She slipped, but caught herself. "I think I'd fall. But thank you for trying to help."

Polly emerged a few minutes later, squeezing through the V-shaped section the exact same way Bic had done, with her chest and back both scraping up against the thick potato skin. If the pathway had no end, they've would've had a terrible time climbing back out again.

"Good spot for a rest?" Bic asked, spreading his arms out.

"Yes," Polly said, looking around. "Yes, it is. I've never walked so far in my entire life. My whole body hurts. And I wish that Great Light up there would turn off for a while. It never stops!"

This new open area was unlike anything they'd come across so far. Everywhere else up until this point had been full of hills, uneven slopes, and dangerous traps—same as the one they'd just climbed through.

"How about over there?" Bic spotted a small cluster of trees only a short walk from where they stood. "We could walk over to that group of Old Earth trees. It should have cooler air. I think it's called 'shielding,' or maybe it's 'shading'? I can't remember. What do you think?"

Polly sat down right where she was. "Right here is fine," she said, crossing her legs and fixing her potato skin covering. Jack of Hearts' potato skin journal was placed gently beside her.

Bic sat down next to her. A rest was long overdue.

Together, they sat in silence and simply stared at Old Earth and all the strange new things it offered.

Trees. Great Light. Sky.

The Old Earth was filled with wonderful things to look at, touch, and feel. Polly nearly laughed with delight as something odd swept past her hot, sweat-lined face. The sensation brought immediate relief and immense pleasure. Something that no resident of Yam Hill had ever experienced.

A cool breeze.

75

During the days of Old Earth, many vessels were created for travel. There were once millions of cars that travelled along on paved roads. The roads still existed, but any unsecured vehicle was lost during the Great Unexpected Tragedy.

People of Old Earth also crafted many types of floating vessels, boats and ships, which could travel great distances across large or small bodies of water.

There were also vessels that carried Old Earth residents through the air. Airplanes, which travelled at incredible speeds, capable of taking people anywhere they wanted to go, not matter how far.

Perhaps the most inventive travel vessel of all was the spacecraft, which could travel high up into the atmosphere. These space vessels travelled higher, faster, and further than any other manmade creation. Some of these space vessels were still, today, travelling through a vast open space, high above Yam Hill.

Residents of Old Earth had travelled into the upper atmosphere, even to "the moon," which Bic and Polly had occasionally seen in magazines, though failed to understand why a large circle in the sky was so important to people of Old Earth.

But there it was—the moon.

Polly spotted it, blending in with the blue background.

76

Among other things, sea life, and all land animals, were decimated by the Great Unexpected Tragedy.

Animal population dropped to zero.

Anything not fastened to the Old Earth, such as water, also departed on that terrible day.

Lakes, rivers, even entire oceans were lost.

Gone in a matter of minutes.

77

Residents of Yam Hill had no pure water.
Potato juice was the only drink.

78

"I could read some of the letter?" Polly said. "If you make us a meal, I could read while we eat."

Bic agreed, but had no new food ideas. Before his illegal Ejection, he'd been experiencing a dry spell for new food ideas. Meals inside Yam Hill may look interesting, but tasted no different.

"I'm not sure I can make one of my special food creations, though." Bic scouted for a good place to dig up their lunch.

"That's fine, Bic," said Polly. "I'm used to eating the same food every day, remember?"

"Okay, good." Bic had already dreamed up a quick yam meal. "I won't be long, okay?"

"Just make sure you come back," Polly said. "I don't want to spend the rest of my life alone. Not here, on Old Earth."

"I promise I'll come back," Bic said. "Even though Old Earth is big, I don't think there's anything here to harm us. It's only the two of us."

Polly doubted that very much. She agreed about it being only them, but not what Bic said about no harm.

The Great Unexpected Tragedy could happen again, at any moment. The Three Elders reminded the people of Yam Hill about this fact constantly, especially during the Community Meetings.

"I'll find a good part to read," Polly said, eager to read the words written inside Jack of Hearts' letter. "There must be at least a few helpful parts in this huge potato scroll. Something in here that can help us survive Old Earth."

"I hope so." Bic walked off to find lunch. It had only been a few hours, not even one full day upon Old Earth, and even his usually outstanding optimism was wearing thin. If they didn't come up with some kind of plan, a means for survival, or a home of some kind, they could be in serious danger.

Survival mode.

While Bic was off preparing their meal, Polly began to unravel Jack of Hearts' enormous potato skin letter. It had been weeks since Polly had taken the time to read anything. But she promised herself that she would not read any of it until Bic returned. But that proved to be much too tempting.

Polly read from the beginning.

My name is Jack of Hearts. I am somewhere between 17 and 19 years old. Eighteen years old is my closest guess. But I could be off by a year or more.

When I was old enough, my mother and father told me that my true name was supposed to be Hearts the Card Game. It was the First Elder who suggested the name Jack of Hearts. And my parents agreed.

I won't bother writing about my parents because they are both Ejected. They both received full honors from the Three Elders. They were good potato residents. I miss them a lot.

I grew up the same as most children of Yam Hill, happy and exploring, wrecking potato furniture, and eating my potato utensils until my parents were angry with me.

They both died when I was young.

Somewhere around eight or nine years old, my father got sick. Then my mother, too. The same day my parents were Ejected, I went to live with the Elders for a short time. They took excellent care of me. Their living quarters are not the same anyone else's. I enjoyed staying there those few months, but I asked if I could go back to my home. They trusted me enough that I could go back to live in my childhood potato home that I loved so much.

Ever since that day, I've been on my own.

When I was strong enough, I went to work for a digging crew. The First Elder helped me get the job. Nobody wanted me to be a digger at first. But when I was 12 or 13 years old, I was already as tall as a lot of the grown men. So they let me dig.

By the time I was sixteen, I was a digging crew lead. I had five other diggers on my team. We mostly had to dig out waste rooms in all the new hallways. That wasn't the most enjoyable work, but I learned a lot.

By the time I was eighteen or nineteen, I had twenty-five people on my digging crew. By the time I was twenty-five, I was the leader of the biggest digging crew in Yam Hill...

"Finding us a good part to read?" Bic hollered.

Polly looked up. "What? Oh. Yes, I am!" Polly was ashamed about reading without Bic there to share the words, so she stopped reading and busied herself with flattening out the rest of the scroll.

The scroll came apart in two separate pieces.

Bic hadn't torn the scroll after all.

"Guess what!" Polly shouted.

"What is it?" Bic was only a short distance away. He finally decided on an untouched area to dig up their lunch meal, kneeling down, scooping up handfuls of yam, busy preparing the best meal he could think up: smashed yams, with tiny sections of dry potato skin for scooping.

"You didn't rip the letter!" Polly told him. "It's two pieces! Jack of Hearts wrote two letters!"

"I didn't tear it?" Bic shouted back. "That's great!" Then he chose a different spot to dig. "Food is almost ready! Need only a short while! I'm just trying to make us some potato juice."

Polly finished spreading out the second scroll, paying close attention to which direction the words were facing. Although she promised herself that she wouldn't read any more, not until Bic returned, one line caught her eyes.

That one line crushed her.

79

Written in Jack of Hearts' neat handwriting was a short line of words that caused Polly's heart to ache worse than anything she'd felt so far.

Four words:

To my daughter, Polly.

80

Inside Yam Hill, there are fathers who raise children to the best of their ability, and love their sons and daughters as if they were their own.

There are also True Fathers.

These are men who not only raise and teach their children to grow up and become respectable potato residents, but are also the biological parent.

Some children have one, two, or no true parents living with them, helping to raise them. All children (at least those currently living) have a male and a female guardian, whether true parent or not.

Both kinds of parents, true or otherwise, take wonderful care of their children.

Bad parenting was a common occurrence during the days of Old Earth, but not inside Yam Hill.

Most received (adopted) children never found out who their true mother or true father was. It sometimes caused too much heartache or sadness. And one of the top priorities of the Three Elders was to keep sadness, confusion, and especially questions about truth-seeking out of the minds of residents.

Potato life had to be kept simple.

81

Children are the most precious commodity.
Potato chips are a close second.

82

When Bic returned a moment later, balancing a potato skin plate of food in one hand and an improvised bowl of potato juice in the other, he found Polly crying.

"Polly, what's wrong?" Bic asked.

Her whole body was shaking as she fought back tears. Not just crying, but gut-wrenching sobs had her practically doubled over in pain.

"What happened?" Bic quickly put the platter of food down, and the bowl of potato juice, then knelt down beside her.

Polly grabbed onto her best friend, squeezing so hard that Bic could hardly breathe. Nowhere near as painful as having a full-grown man standing on his ribcage (as Amadeus had done, unknowingly, back inside Jack of Hearts' room), though he was still quite tender there.

Bic held onto her, not knowing what else he could do. Although he was unsure of the reason for this full body embrace, he certainly wasn't going to refuse.

"Are you hurt?" Bic asked. "What is it?"

Over the top of Polly's shoulder, Bic could easily read the large inscribed words that had made his best friend so upset. There, at the top of the second piece of potato skin scroll, written much earlier than the other words, and much more legible.

Bic had to read the words several times to fully understand their meaning. Seeing those words, reading them over again, he couldn't help but wonder whether his own mother and father—the two people he always assumed brought him into Yam Hill—were his true mother and true father.

Polly was the one he was worried about now.

"Jack of Hearts was your true father?" Bic was still trying to process this information. "I had no idea. Although, after he cut off all his hair and his beard, he did look more like you. A lot like you."

Polly gave up wiping her tears away. She let them fall, not caring anymore.

Bic wasn't so hungry anymore.

"My parents—" Polly stopped. In an angry voice, she said, "The people who have been raising me, not my true parents, have been lying to me. They've lied to me for my entire life."

Bic had to think. Even if Polly was a child of reception, not a true child, her parents had done an excellent job of raising her. Polly's parents were not liars. If anything, the Three Elders had forced Polly's parents to keep the truth hidden all these years.

"No, Polly," Bic said, pulling away but not letting go of her. "Your mother and father have not been lying to you. They did a great job of raising you. It's not them, Polly. It's the—" He looked away, unable to say it.

"What?" Polly asked, the tears finally receding.

"The Three Elders have been lying," Bic finally said. "Not your parents. The Three Elders have been lying to everyone inside Yam Hill."

It felt good to get the truth out, though he did feel ashamed for saying the words out loud. He was raised to believe that the Elders, past and present, were extraordinary men. Not liars and hypocrites.

"Maybe that's what he wanted to tell you," Bic said, wishing to change the subject.

"Who? Jack of Hearts?" Polly said. "I mean, my true father?"

"Yes," Bic said. "You told me that Jack of Hearts came to visit you a few days ago. That he had something important to tell you, remember?"

"He did," Polly said, wiping at her face. She could still hear his voice, shouting as the Three Elders and his co-worker, Amadeus, forcefully Ejected him. Those thoughts, she hoped, would be pushed away and be replaced with thoughts of his kind, compassionate ways and his wonderful smile.

"I'll bet that's it," Bic said. "He was going to explain that he was your true father."

Knowing the truth felt good. But Polly's insides still reeled because not only did she not know this all along, but also that she would never again be able to enjoy his company, or have one of their long talks.

Polly was soon calm enough that she was breathing normally. She was drawing shapes in the outer potato skin with her fingers, most of which had no fingernails. They'd been ripped out while she was being dragged through half of Yam Hill by the First Elder.

Bic leaned over and brought the potato skin plates closer to each of them.

"Do you think you can eat something?" Bic asked.

Polly wanted to say no, but agreed that she could. If she didn't eat something soon, her body would begin to fail.

"Not bad," Polly said, taking a bite of Bic's yam creation. "Didn't you make this one night when I came over for supper a few weeks ago?"

Bic thought a moment, then shook his head. "No, I don't think so. This is one of my new food ideas. The taste is the same— yams, of course. But I think the tiny bits of potato skin add a bit of different texture. And they're fun to scoop with."

"It's good." Polly's stomach seemed to thank her, though she was force-feeding herself.

After only a small meal, both of them lay down for what was supposed to be a short rest. The sun was directly overhead, but the potato cliffs they'd just climbed through provided them with some reprieve and kept them out of its direct light.

As they laid there, nothing was spoken, but plenty was said between them. Bic was glad he was not alone. So was Polly, and made that clear by inching closer to Bic and burrowing up beside him.

Polly quietly cried herself to sleep.

Bic's mind raced, but sleep soon overtook him. And this time there were dreams. Dreams of being taken over, or possibly chased.

83

Dreams aren't always simply dreams.
Sometimes they're a warning.

84

Insomnia is a non-issue for residents of Yam Hill. During the days of Old Earth, medicines were prescribed for those having trouble falling asleep. Such a problem did not exist for people inside the potato, for many reasons. Without an onslaught of daily worries, sleep comes naturally.

People ate when they were hungry, slept when they were tired, and carried out their daily potato lives in a calm, sedentary, carefree lifestyle. Aside from the occasional worry about what time to eat, or where the nearest waste room was (if travelling), there were no day-to-day worries.

Without schedules to keep, or working for the sole purpose of paying off debts, residents could enjoy life, such as it is…inside a giant potato.

Eat. Sleep. Read. Repeat.

This was the unwritten motto of Yam Hill, the lifestyle of the common people. And the Three Elders worked very hard to keep it that way.

85

Aside from Diggers, and perhaps Light Checkers, especially when a well-travelled hallway or staircase ever went completely dark (which did happen on occasion, forcing mandatory long work hours), no resident of Yam Hill ever experienced true exhaustion.

Polly and Bic fell asleep, exhausted.

They slept as the sun passed overhead. Both of them continued to sleep as the sun began to settle behind the rows of tall trees in the distance.

If Bic hadn't been startled awake by Polly's snoring, they might have slept until full dark. If that happened, they might've been caught.

Completely off-guard.

Easy targets.

86

"POLLY!"

With her heartbeat racing, Polly quickly sat up, ready to deal with whatever critical situation was happening. Her initial reaction was that Bic was hurt.

Looking around, she saw Bic seated next to her, perfectly at ease, not concerned at all. He was sitting cross-legged, snacking on some cold yam from the meal he'd prepared for them earlier.

"Why are you yelling?" Polly snapped. "I thought something was wrong."

Bic swallowed and said, "Hm? No, nothing is wrong. You're just hard to wake up. I've called your name at least twenty times, louder and louder." With a smile, he added, "And you snored, *again*."

Polly stretched her arms to the side. She yawned, and when her hand was finished covering her mouth, a fist was made, which was then used to make solid contact with Bic's right arm.

"Careful!" Bic said, rubbing his arm. "That hurt."

"Good," Polly said. "That was for scaring me awake. I thought we were being attacked. Or that you fell off a cliff and had another one of those trees stuck in your side again."

Although he didn't enjoy the physical abuse, he was glad to see that Polly was acting more like her usual feisty self. The sad version of Polly was not seen often, but Bic certainly did not blame her for the prolonged sadness. A lot had happened during the last day.

"What happened to the Great Light?" Polly asked, reaching for some more of Bic's yam creation. She woke up starving. "I enjoy this much light a lot better. That other bright light is almost too much for my eyes to understand."

Bic stood up and surveyed their situation. For a long time, he didn't say anything, simply looked one way, then the other, and back again.

"Don't think too hard," Polly said with a smirk. "You might burst."

"Funny, Polly." Bic was trying to decide on a direction. What few stories he'd read about how Old Earth actually worked, the best he could come up with was that they had a short time of daylight left, then complete darkness for a while, followed by another Great Light appearance at some point in the future.

"I can't decide which is the better way to go," Bic finally said. "From what I remember, Old Earth is round. Same as the Great Light. I think they move around each other, sort of in a full circle. Or does Old Earth move around the sun?" He couldn't remember.

"I have no idea, Bic," Polly said. "But I do know that you better eat some of this, or I'm going to eat the whole thing."

"Go ahead," Bic told her. "I'm not hungry. But I do think we need to keep moving. We should get as far as we can before the sunlight goes completely dark on us. I have a feeling that…"

Polly waited while Bic sorted out his thoughts.

"What feeling?" Polly asked. "You need to use the waste room? Take a look around, Bic. There are no waste rooms. This is Old Earth. I think, if you need to, you can bring relief anywhere."

"No, not that," Bic said, not embarrassed in the least. "I was thinking about which direction we should go. They all look the same to me."

"Well, I'm going to the waste room then," Polly said, then walked off and chose a spot. She was back in a few minutes, standing beside Bic, looking around, seeing exactly what he saw.

Trees.

Steep slopes in all directions.

"We're lost, aren't we?" Polly said.

"No, we're not lost, Polly," said Bic, sounding optimistic. "I just think we need to find a direction. Lost is when you can't find your way. We just need to choose the right path."

She bumped him. "Is that supposed to make sense?"

Bic laughed. "Come on, let's go."

With hardly anything to pack up, only Jack of Hearts' letter to carry, the two of them headed off in relatively the same direction as before. With only an hour or two of light remaining, Bic pushed hard to get them as far along as possible before travel became too treacherous in the dark.

Less than an hour's walk from where they'd taken an afternoon rest, Bic and Polly decided to stop. They would spend the night sheltered in between two tall potato skin peaks, hidden from view. This unplanned act turned out to save both their lives.

"In the morning, I'll make us a proper breakfast," Bic said, digging his fingers in and peeling back a section of potato skin. "Then, if we have enough of the Great Light, we can hopefully make it to the bottom of Yam Hill."

"I hope so," Polly said, sitting down and getting as comfortable as she could on the uneven ground.

Bic was content just sitting next to Polly. Their situation, exploring Old Earth, had brought them even closer together. All they had was each other, and that was enough for now.

"Do you think you can read some more?" Bic asked. He didn't want to upset her further, but he was curious about what Jack of Hearts had written down.

"Let's see what I can find..." Polly spread the letter out in front of her, glancing over the words, searching for anything that caught her eye. She wanted to find something about Old Earth, some section that might actually help them.

"Is there anything in the letter about the Great Unexpected Tragedy?" Bic asked, wiping a bit of yam from the corner of his mouth. "Maybe Jack of Hearts wrote something about what actually happened all those years ago. The Elders always give hints at the monthly meetings, but they never tell us anything about what it was really like, other than it was the worst thing that ever happened in the history of everything."

Polly was quiet while she searched.

The great open space above their heads was changing from blue to dark blue, but there was still enough light to read by.

"Right here! Found it!" Polly pointed excitedly at the letter.

Bic saw the words too, written in very large letters, carved in Jack of Hearts' surprisingly neat handwriting.

"This is it," Polly said. "This will be the true version of what happened. Not filled with lies from the Three Elders."

Great. Unexpected. Tragedy.

Three words that all residents of Yam Hill knew by heart, but rarely spoke out loud because of the very realistic fear that history would repeat itself.

88

Underneath those three terrible words was an explanation from the author, Jack of Hearts.

Polly read his words out loud.

89

Every day, the Three Elders gather in the living room of Mr. Yamhill's house and read from his old journal. I have sat with them many times over the years and listened to the story. That is why I have the first part of the history of Yam Hill memorized.

After a huge first meal of the day, which I often cook for them, with eggs and meat along with fried yams, they each take turns reading from its pages.

The journal itself is not very long. It's only about fifteen pages in total. I've never actually held the journal myself, in my own hands. But that's what the Elders told me when I asked them. It's short, but very detailed. Equally disturbing and sad.

The words are written in an Old Earth book of white paper. The pages are similar to the paper inside all the Elder-approved books that get passed around to residents of Yam Hill. Those books once belonged to Mr. Yamhill himself.

Mr. Yamhill has many books in his house. Hundreds of books. Most of them have been read and approved by the Elders. Other books are not allowed inside Yam Hill because they explain too much.

Anything written inside a book or magazine that will encourage questions, or challenge what the Elders tell people, they won't allow to leave the house.

Myself, I have read a few of these books. I am permitted to take them with me during my outings for the Elders. I read them outside of Yam Hill, where no one would ever find me. Even though I am a trusted employee for the Three Elders, I am strictly forbidden from bringing a non-approved book into Yam Hill.

What I discovered in these books was that people of Old Earth were very creative people. They invented many wonderful things. It would take thousands of pages to write down everything the people of Old Earth made.

But they were also very destructive people. And very protective people. They guarded themselves heavily, from many things. They even guarded themselves from other people.

But with all their intelligence, and all their fancy inventions, nothing could protect them from what happened. Nothing could have saved them.

Mr. Yamhill's journal talks mainly about the day gravity stopped working. When all those people from all over the world, all those lives, up and drifted away. Something called gravity was the invisible force that Old Earth people believed held them down and stopped them from floating away.

Mr. Yamhill did not believe in gravity.

When Old Earth was safe, long before the Great Unexpected Tragedy, Mr. Yamhill worked as an electricity expert. Sort of how Light Checkers working inside Yam Hill keep all the LED lights in the hallways working, and all the lights inside everyone's potato homes working properly.

Mr. Yamhill had a great knowledge about electricity and how to keep it working all the time. His brilliant ideas about electricity even helped him rescue his neighbors while everyone else around him was floating up to their terrible loss of life.

Mr. Yamhill thought people and things were not bound to Old Earth by some gravity force pulling them down. He thought people and things stayed close to the ground because of electricity — not gravity.

I'm not exactly sure how it all works, but he believed that an electrical magnet lived inside every person. And that people were made up of energy, and electricity, and that the force pulling all of us down is inside us. This electrical magnet force kept people, basically everything, from floating into the air.

Then one day, when nobody in all the world expected it, the electricity magnets holding everyone down, it all suddenly stopped working right.

All over the world this happened, killing everyone. It failed everywhere except inside Yam Hill.

Inside Yam Hill, people were safe and did not float away. Electricity kept them bound to Old Earth, but only if they stayed inside the yam.

Although Mr. Yamhill's words will never be read by any resident of Yam Hill, most of what the Elders have told everyone about the Great Unexpected Tragedy is true.

Every single living person, all over the world, their feet suddenly left Old Earth. They simply floated away. Not just people, but every single object that was not attached to Old Earth or secured tightly. All those things simply floated up in to the air and were never seen again.

What the Elders don't tell anyone is that it's finished. It's all over. Electricity, all those magnets and inside forces pulling us down, they started working again.

At some point, a long time ago, Old Earth returned to normal. Everything started working properly again.

Life has been restored. Old Earth is safe once again. People will not disappear into the air the moment they step onto the Old Earth.

But because of the secrets that began with the previous Elders, the secrets grew worse every year. Those secrets turned into lies. And lies that were told for a long time, people began to believe they were proper truth.

Old Earth is safe. That is truth, I promise you.

The current Elders, same as all the Elders before them, and the Elders before them, don't want to believe it. They don't want to change. They don't want to take the chance that it could happen again. That is why life continues the way it does inside Yam Hill.

Could the Great Unexpected Tragedy happen again?

Yes.

It could happen again. But that does not mean all residents, everyone living inside Yam Hill, shouldn't go outside and try to live again on Old Earth.

Before that happens, the proper truth must be told.

The current Elders, men I've known for a long time, are simply carrying on what those first Elders started to do. They lie to protect themselves. So they can continue their way of life. A much more comfortable life than anyone else living inside Yam Hill. They continue to shut people out, and keep residents from understanding Old Earth.

mr. Yamhill's journal exposes the truth. What amazes me the most is that the words are just as legible now as when they were written, about five decades ago...

90

Polly stopped and looked up. "What's leg-ible? Something to do with our legs?"

Bic leaned in closer to look at the word. "No, not legs. I think it has something to do with how we read words. If they make sense or not."

Polly tried to find her spot again. The light was growing weaker all around them. She turned around and put her back to the Great Light, with the letter facing the sun, which helped.

"What was that other part?" Bic asked. "The part about when the words were written."

Polly scanned the letter, found the spot, then read the words again.

"It says 'the words are just as legible now as when they were written about five decades ago'."

Bic had a confused look on his dirty face.

"What's wrong with that?" Polly asked.

"A lot is wrong with that, Polly," Bic said. "What have the Elders always told us? About Yam Hill, and how old it is? That Yam Hill is—"

"—hundreds and hundreds of years old," Polly said, mindlessly finishing the well-known phrase.

"Exactly. The Elders say those same exact words at least a couple of times during every Community Meeting," Bic went on. "But if Jack of Hearts is telling the truth in his letter..."

Polly looked irritated. "Jack of Hearts had no reason—" She stopped, then said, "I mean, my true father had no reason to lie. His letter is telling us the truth, Bic."

"I know that," Bic went on, taking no offense. "That's what I'm trying to say, Polly. If Jack of Hearts is right, and the Elders have been lying to us about the Great Unexpected Tragedy, then our entire history is wrong."

"Why?" Polly asked. "How is it wrong?"

"A decade is ten years, Polly," said Bic. "That means Yam Hill is only fifty years old."

"So...half of one century?" Polly was unsure of the exact timeline, but that sounded right.

"Yes, Polly," Bic said. "That means not only have the Elders been lying to us about Old Earth, and how it's not a safe place to live, they've also been lying about how long people have been living inside Yam Hill."

"Are you surprised?" Polly asked him.

Bic replied with a simple and hurt, "Yes."

Polly looked down. "Sorry, Bic. I didn't mean to say that so harsh. I'm surprised, too. Even though Jack of Hearts has been telling me the truth, or at least *trying* to tell me as much truth as he could, I suppose nobody had any reason to not believe the Elders."

Bic wasn't mad at Polly. After all, she had never lied to him.

"Fifty years is still a long time," Bic went on, "but not even close to the 'hundreds and hundreds' of years they always tell us."

"That's why we all believe it," Polly said. "Because the Elders say it so often. I've heard that same lie since I was a kid."

"Exactly," Bic said. "When I was a kid, I always tried to imagine what Old Earth looked like hundreds, or even thousands of years ago. Now I find out the Elders, the three people in Yam Hill that everyone is supposed to trust and look up to, are just like Jack of Hearts said...they're liars."

"And hypocrites," Polly said, liking the way the word sounded. She wasn't entirely certain what it meant, but remembered Jack of Hearts saying it, so it must be unkind.

"I don't know about that part," Bic said, "but I'm sure Jack of Hearts had a reason for saying that. I think it means saying one thing, then doing something else." He took a moment to look around at all the trees with their brilliant greens, and the great blue sky above, enjoying the wonderful crisp air available to them.

So much beautiful truth.

So many horrible lies.

"I can't believe Old Earth has been safe for people to return," Bic said, "and the Elders kept it a secret this whole time. Why would they do that?"

Polly didn't know. She asked if he wanted to hear any more, or if he'd heard enough truth for one night.

"Is there any more about the Great Unexpected Tragedy?" Bic asked. "Does Jack of Hearts explain any of that? What happened to all those people?"

Polly scanned the letter, forced to turn it in several directions to make out the etched words in the fading light.

"Yes, right here," Polly said, using a finger to hold her spot. "It's getting too dark to read, but I'll do my best." She held out the letter to Bic. "Here, you read the letter. You're much faster at reading words than I am."

"No." Bic smiled. "I enjoy listening to your voice. I've known you my whole life, but this is the most I've ever heard you read."

Polly made herself comfortable, then leaned in close to Jack of Hearts' letter. Then she read aloud the words that no resident of Yam Hill was supposed to hear.

91

Polly read the true history of Old Earth.

Mr. Yamhill's words, as remembered by Jack of Hearts.

92

When gravity stopped working, I was out in my garden. I was testing out some new plant food on my little patch of potatoes. Since I've lived my entire life here in beautiful Idaho, I figured in my retirement I should at least attempt to grow some potatoes.

This was my second year with the yams. For those not in the know, yes, there is a difference between a yam and a sweet potato. But as far as I'm concerned, they've been one and the same since I was a kid, so I'll stick with calling them yams.

Funny how it's also part of my name.

My full name is Raymond Yamhill. I represent one of the fifty-eight survivors. Everyone else is gone. Earth's population in next to zilch.

I remember feeling very content that day, even happy, even though it was this time last year that Hazel, my wife of 42 years, suddenly passed away.

It was summertime, first week of the season. The day was gorgeous, not a cloud in the sky.

Then I heard Mrs. Halter scream.

When I peeked around the side of my house and looked over her way, she was floating up into the air like a balloon. First, she seemed to hover near the roof of her house. Then she was forty feet in the air. Then a hundred feet. And she just kept going. Head over heels, up she went. Her little dog, Clarabelle, was right there with her. Poor thing was barking its little fool head off as she went up, no idea what was going on.

It wasn't just Mrs. Halter, my neighbor from across the street. It was happening everywhere.

Gravity just up and quit.

From where I stood in my backyard, I could see hundreds, if not thousands of tiny black dots rising into the air. Up to the clouds, then gone. Out of sight.

I hadn't slept well the night before, so maybe in my tired state it took a while for the reality part to kick in.

Those tiny black dots were people.

I remember standing on my tip-toes, trying to see better. Trying to figure out what in the world I could do to help. In the process, I knocked over the entire bucket of super-grow plant food I was testing out on my yams.

Then it was my turn.

Good thing my reflexes are still in working order, because as soon as my own two feet left the ground, I held on to that garden hose for all of life's worth. That was the only thing that saved me, I believe.

Thank goodness I opted for the expensive hose. Hazel wanted me to buy the one on sale, but I fought her on it. And thank goodness. Otherwise it might've ripped clear away from the house, then I would've floated up into the atmosphere along with everyone else.

After a good long struggle, probably twenty minutes or more, I was finally able to pull myself close to the house, then finally into a standing position.

Now I know what the astronauts went through.

Finally, I made it into the house. And what a sight that was! When I pulled myself in through the sliding glass door, everything that should've been stayed put, was up on the ceiling, sort of dancing around. But I made it safely into the house.

Those first couple of nights were the worst.

There was plenty of water and food in the house. It was just a matter of getting to it. Eating wasn't so bad. But drinking a bottle of water while you're upside-down, or spinning in circles is not my idea of fun. And I'd rather not mention trips to the bathroom.

What surprised me most was that one of the TV news stations was still on the air. That station ran for about a day after the event, when the whole world went topsy-turvy.

Some scared young news reporter found a way to strap himself down and managed to deliver the news. But all he could do was tell us what we already knew. That gravity had stopped working, and that people were dying. He talked a lot about the suicides. How people shouldn't just give up. That gravity might be restored soon.

But even he went off the air by the second day. Then it was nothing. TV didn't work anymore. All electricity was unavailable. Thank goodness the sun still worked, otherwise any survivors, myself included, wouldn't have been able to see enough to move around.

All communication had been wiped out. In a matter of less than forty-eight hours, we went back to the dark ages.

That entire first week was a blur.

I just floated around the house, thinking up different ideas. Life couldn't go on like this, but I wasn't about to end my life prematurely.

The suicides got worse every day.

I watched them from my front window. No more than a handful of seconds would pass before another black dot in the sky would float up and out of sight. Or in a group, all of them holding hands, which I imagine were entire families deciding to make their exit together. Broke my heart every time I saw it. I wanted to turn my head each time it happened, but most times I couldn't look away.

Suicide is not in my DNA, but I certainly couldn't spend my golden years floating around, slurping food out of the air, and sleeping on the ceiling.

Somewhere around day eight, a miracle happened. I received an answer to my prayers.

My normal life was restored because of a giant potato.

I still clearly recall that afternoon, when my little yam from the garden basically swallowed my house. I was up near the ceiling, having fallen asleep, probably with my nose pressed up against the ceiling again. Even though it was getting late, there was still enough sunlight peeking through the windows.

A loud noise woke me up.

When I finally floated my way towards the back of the house to see what had happened, all I could see was a solid wall of yam. My little backyard potatoes were now bigger than my house.

The next crash, an hour or two later, was the storage shed being swallowed up. My little yam wasn't so little anymore. And it just kept growing. These were the tiny little yams from my garden in the backyard. I didn't know if it was one yam, or two, or a thousand of them.

Not until much later did we find out it was just one. And that one yam was so big that it completely took over my house. And then the shed. And then every inch of backyard that I could see.

By the end of the following day, the only window I could still see out of was the living room window.

That night I hit the floor. Everything else came crashing down around me. Good thing nothing too heavy was nearby. Our old washer and dryer combo from downstairs had somehow made its way into the living room, where I was at the time. That big hunk of metal came crashing down right beside me. I'd hate to think what would've happened if it came right down on top of me. The outcome might've been much different. Or all the sharps knives, pens and pencils, or broken glass I could've landed on.

There I was, with my feet back on the ground. My first reaction was that everything was back to normal. That the world had returned to the way it was before. Or at least that so-called gravity had been restored, and life would resume as before.

No. Just me.

Everything outside was still a mess. Those black dots, all those people, were still floating up into the sky. I must've stood there for more than twenty minutes, counting. I counted to just shy of one hundred, then I had to walk away.

Now that things had returned to normal, at least for me, that's when I really put my thinking cap on. My thinking boots, you could say.

People were dying out there, and I wanted to help. I wanted to save as many of them as I possibly could. Those were men, women, and children out there.

Finally, after racking my poor old brain, I came up with an idea that just might work. If it didn't work, I'd be dead right now instead of writing all this down. I just wish it hadn't taken me all that time, probably two or three days to come up with my plan.

Once I had a plan, it worked better than I expected.

I made up my artificial gravity boots in less than an hour.

Working as an electrician for nearly forty-five years, I think it's safe to say that I learned a thing or two about electricity. All I needed was some iron, which I found in the basement, some copper wire, and a battery. I had plenty of hardware in the garage, lots of iron bolts, and spools of wire. And since my wife's car had crashed back down to Earth, I was able to pull the battery out. My old truck was parked outside on the driveway when gravity stopped working, so it was long gone.

Soon I was decked out in my new boots. Although things had returned to normal inside my house, thanks to a giant yam, the world outside was still a gravity-free zone. It took a little practice with the boots, but soon I felt confident enough to make my first trip.

Then off I went, through the neighborhood.

I'm sure I must've been quite the sight with all those iron bolts and copper wire tied around my ankles, lugging around that big car battery.

The charge was weak, but it worked. My rigged up boots provided just enough magnetic force to keep me down.

What a wonderful feeling when Don, my neighbor, saw me walking over to his house. He'd never looked so happy. I handed him the rope I brought along with me, and told him to make a knot, good and tight. Then I pulled him all the way home. Carried him just like a kid with a balloon.

Then I did it again. And again, and again.

Fifty-seven times I did this same trick. Took about a day and a half to collect everyone. Basically, everyone I could get to without sacrificing anybody's safety.

Everyone else was gone. But none of that mattered. We had fifty-eight people, myself included, inside my house. Survivors of the worst natural disaster in recorded history.

Well—the second worst disaster, I suppose, including the Great Flood. There were only eight survivors for that, so I guess we had it better than old Noah.

To think about all those women and children who didn't make it. That still rips my heart to pieces every time I think about it.

All those billions of people, simply gone.

Last I heard, Earth was already past the seven billion mark. Now, as far as we know, it's down to 58.

Now wait a minute. Let me back up.

I made a comment before about something called gravity. This is a bit of an issue with me, since I don't exactly believe in this manmade theory called the Force of Gravity.

Call me crazy. Call me whatever suits your need. But over card games and Sunday morning coffee, I've tried to talk to several of my friends, grown men and women, about even the remote possibility that gravity isn't what they think it is. How it's a made-up theory and not a real force at all.

Every single one of them got mad at me. And I mean they got mad as a hornet when I tried to explain how gravity might not even exist. I'd bring up the idea started by that Tesla fellow, called electromagnetic force, and how that's the force keeping us all pinned down to the Earth's surface.

Not one person, and I mean not one of them wanted to hear it. Especially Mrs. Halter from across the street.

One night she invited me over to dinner to meet her daughter and her new husband. Adrian, her son-in-law, was the only one open to the idea of electromagnetism. And feisty old Mrs. Halter, I thought at one point she was going to get up from the table and hit me. I'd probably laugh about that strange evening now—if things were different, of course. Not when my last memory of Mrs. Halter, which is still fresh in my mind, was how I watched her float up into the sky, yelling for help that I was unable to give.

No. I am not a big believer of gravity. I am more of an electromagnetic fan, myself. Even as a kid, gravity sounded like a funny idea to me. But I was forced to believe in it, for a very long time. Because everyone told me I had to. Then I grew up, read a lot of books, and came to my own conclusion.

We've all heard the phrase "ball of energy" and that people are made up of physical atoms, and atoms are nothing but energy. Even old Einstein himself said that energy cannot be destroyed, it can only change shape. That stands to reason that if people all over the earth are nothing but pure energy, why in the world shouldn't we be stuck to the earth through electricity?

We are, I believe.

But what happens when that force up and quits?

Then we're all in big trouble.

As I write these words, sitting here comfortably inside my living room, looking outside my dusty widow, it almost looks as if nothing is wrong out there.

But the world outside is a mess.

It's been hardly over a month since the world's population up and headed for outer space. Everyone around here has been calling it The Great Unexpected Tragedy.

Nothing out there is alive.

If anyone dares to step outside this house, they'll be swept up into the air like all those other poor, helpless people.

My house is the only safe spot. I'm not exactly sure how, or why, but inside the yam we're all walking around like normal. We're all busy trying to adapt to this new life. Life inside this giant potato.

Which brings me to the yam.

There's not much I can explain because none of us can leave this giant potato. We can't even step outside to see how big it's gotten these last few weeks. Not unless they want to suffer the same fate as all those other billions of people.

Yam Hill is already the size of a mountain.

My neighbor, Don, volunteered to go outside at the end of the third week. We made damn sure we weren't going to lose him. He had enough rope around his waist to stretch halfway across Idaho. And he had about fifteen people holding onto that rope, stretching from the living room all the way to the kitchen.

Now, he didn't get the best look outside. He was out there for less than a minute. And most of that was spent trying to get him back inside the house.

But he saw enough. As soon as he yelled, we brought him back inside. We shut the door and locked it. And that door hasn't been opened since.

People are retreating into the yam. They're building shelters, carving out rooms, and getting settled in this strange new home of ours.

My house is quite large, five bedrooms, plus the finished basement. But it's nowhere near big enough to sleep fifty-eight people.

That's where the yam comes in.

People have taken to calling it Yam Hill, named after me. At first, I didn't much like the idea, but everyone else seems to like it, so Yam Hill it is.

And once we got electricity up and running again, everyone seemed much better off.

I'm an electrician by trade. Been working with electricity all my life. And I'm certain that somewhere along the way, I heard or read somewhere that you can make electricity using a potato. Not until I found myself living inside a giant potato did the idea occur to me. But now that I've tried it, and taught the others how to make it work, potato electricity is an absolute wonder.

Everything needed to light up the yam, I've got in large quantity out in my storage shed. As you can imagine, I've accumulated a lot of electrical supplies over my forty-plus years of running a business.

People have taken to digging. They're out there day and night, making tunnels, and clearing walkways. We now have access to my shed, and all those electrical supplies.

All the light inside Yam Hill is certainly making life easier. The only natural light we get comes through my living room window. Thank the heavens that the sun didn't up and quit, too.

Life on the outside might be ruined, but we're all working together to get through this. The hardest part is to forget about going outside. Back to what people around here are already calling Old Earth.

This yam of ours just keeps on getting bigger.

There are constant noises coming from outside. Lots of shifting, day and night. Sounds a bit like an earthquake, I imagine, though I've never experienced an earthquake.

Growing pains, you could say. By the sound of it, Yam Hill continues to grow bigger every day. None of us have any idea just how big it's gotten. That's because none of us are stupid enough to go outside and check. Going outside would be the last trip you ever took.

All we can do right now is hope and pray that there are more people out there. More survivors. People all over the world must've come up with a similar idea to mine. There must be more survivors out there.

We may never know for sure, but I'd sure like to think there are hundreds, thousands, maybe even hundreds of thousands of people left. Enough so that we can start over...

93

Mr. Yamhill was wrong. Only his group survived.
World Population: zero.
Idaho: 58.

94

"I can't read any more," Polly said. "It's too dark to see the words."

"That's fine," Bic told her. "You read really well."

Polly smiled. "Thank you, Bic."

"Besides being too dark," Bic said. "I'm not sure I can listen to any more. Living through the Great Unexpected Tragedy must've been horrible. Glad I wasn't there to see it."

Polly agreed. "I don't think I want to hear any more, either. The history of Old Earth is worse than I thought. It must've been terrible what all those people went through. How many is seven billion?"

Bic tried to think of a number that high, but couldn't imagine it. "I'm not sure, Polly. I think, probably so many people that nobody can count that big."

Polly thought about Mr. Yamhill, and how he had to watch all those tiny black dots—all those people—ascending into the air, helpless.

"How many people do we have living inside Yam Hill?" Polly asked.

"Six hundred and four," Bic quickly recited. That specific number, whatever the current number of Yam Hill residents happens to be, is usually memorized by most residents. The Elders always said it, numerous times, during every Community Meeting.

"Wrong, Bic," Polly said. "Six hundred and two."

Bic took a second. "Oh. Right. Minus us."

"At least back then they had Mr. Yamhill," Polly said. "Sounds like he was a brave man."

Bic absolutely agreed. "Our Elders might lie to us, but it sounds like Mr. Yamhill truly was a brilliant man. He even shared his home with all the original survivors. The part about his one little yam growing big and swallowing up his house was amazing. I always thought Yam Hill was this big already."

Nearly fifty years later, Yam Hill was still growing.

Polly leaned back and stretched her stiff muscles. While reading Jack of Hearts' letter, she'd been sitting cross-legged, with her nose getting closer and closer to the words as their primary light source faded. She was still holding the letter in her lap when Bic spotted something.

"What's that part?" Bic asked. He was the one to notice the words scribbled across the potato skin parchment.

Polly's shoulder popped, leaning in. "Which part are you talking about? This?"

"Right there, under your right hand." Bic pointed to a group of words below where Polly had left off. The words were larger than all the others, scratched across nearly the entire page, written over top of other words.

"I am..." Polly turned the letter sideways.

Polly read:

AMADEUS IS COMING

95

Polly fell asleep first.

Bic stayed up half the night, thinking about their situation and how they would survive. He stared up at the dark sky, with its amazing spread of tiny lights, and tried very hard to not worry about the future. If, that is, Old Earth could even provide them any kind of future together.

Polly snored softly.

Bic smiled in the dark. Although he also required rest, he loved the way Polly looked as she slept, a silhouette on the dark ground. She was so peaceful, knees pulled up to her chest, breathing softly.

If they were to travel the next day, or whenever the Great Light showed up again, or if it showed up again, Bic would also need to be rested. Even a few hours' sleep would be a gift.

Rolling over on his side, Bic closed his eyes.

Still, in his worried mind there were flashing images of all the magazine pages he'd seen. Old pictures with great sheets of cold white covering everything. He understood some of how Old Earth used to work, and that at some point during the year, a great coldness takes over the land. Great sheets of white powder and ice cover Old Earth, freezing everything. Including living things.

Tonight, the night air was sufficiently warm. Otherwise Bic would've stayed up the rest of the dark hours to craft Polly a new potato skin blanket so at least she could be warm. He guessed they must be in the warm cycle, where Old Earth was heated by the Great Light, before it leaves and all the land freezes over.

Bic yawned.

Inching his way right up right next to Polly, he did not feel ashamed to put his arm around her. His best friend, and co-survivor, did not mind either. Polly shifted in her sleep, then pulled Bic tighter.

Bic knew he'd be able to sleep. Some, at least.

The strange words scribbled on the potato skin letter passed through his mind, but exited quickly. Hardly any of the last two, three, maybe even four or five hours of critical thinking was wasted worrying about the words carved across Jack of Hearts' letter.

Jack of Hearts was dead.

Amadeus, the huge hairy man with the crazy smile, was hard at work inside Yam Hill, probably digging new tunnels and stairwells, or busy working for the Three Elders.

No one was coming after them.

They were all alone, which was both good and bad. Bic loved being with Polly, whom he considered his equal. It was just the two of them. But they would need help to survive, or at least some guidance. They simply could not carry on like this, wandering aimlessly throughout Old Earth.

Bic understood the intent was to get to the bottom of Yam Hill. Those were the directions Jack of Hearts had shouted at them while he was being Ejected.

But then what?

Bic yawned again.

If they did not find some shelter, or dig out a new potato home, life would carry on this way. Endless travelling, with no clear direction. And eventually, after all ideas had failed, out of desperation, they would probably climb back up Yam Hill, to the Ejection Site, and beg to be let back in.

Polly made a noise in her throat, dreaming.

No matter what happened on Old Earth, Bic knew that Polly would be there in the morning. That was the thought that triggered his brain to stop thinking so hard, stop worrying so much, and concentrate on what was good.

Eventually, he too fell asleep. This time outside Yam Hill, on its hard, outer skin instead of both of them inside their potato rooms, sleeping on their soft, comfortable beds made of sculpted yam.

96

The rifle blast woke them up.
Amadeus had found them.

97

"Polly, wake up!" Bic shouted. "We're being attacked!"

No time for a proper wake-up.

No time for breakfast.

No time to stretch stiff limbs.

It was time to run.

Amadeus had fired one shot already, but missed. But his aim was getting better each time he fired the Old Earth rifle.

98

For most of the desperate journey, Bic stayed in the lead. This role reversal was fun at first, even confidence-building. For the first time in their long relationship, he was in charge.

Bic quickly realized that being in charge was not so great, especially with a madman chasing after them. Decisions had to be made. Tough decisions that sometimes involved an argument.

"At some point, I think we need to climb down, Polly," Bic would remind her. "We can't just keep running away from him, staying on this same flat path."

"What path?" Polly snapped. "That Amadeus man is trying to end our lives, Bic. He's blasting that awful noisemaker at us, that Old Earth tool."

Rushing through another overgrown patch of Yam Hill, Polly accepted her co-survivors hand as he helped pull her up and over another fallen tree.

Occasionally, sometimes as often as every couple of minutes, a rifle blast, or angry shouting—or both—could be heard somewhere behind them. Sometimes it sounded as if Amadeus was near enough that they would turn around and see him.

Unknown to Polly and Bic, he was alarmingly close.

Amadeus had them in his sight on more than one occasion over the last few hours—eye sight, and also in the sight of his rifle. Each time he'd gotten that close, it turned out he'd chosen the wrong path. A thick patch of trees, or some overgrowth would deter him, block his clear shot. Then he'd be forced to backtrack, or find a new path, or make his own.

Polly and Bic could hear his awful voice, never too far behind. Always threatening, but in such a polite manner.

"I'm sorry I have to kill you both!" Amadeus would shout, or "I'm only doing my job!"

More than once they'd heard him shout, "Please stop running and I promise to kill you peacefully!"

Polly and Bic ignored him, and ran.

99

By themselves, Polly and Bic were each able to climb down most of the smaller ledges and minor cliffs. Many were no taller than the length of two people. Some of the smaller ledges, Bic was able to slide down while favoring his injured ankle.

Other drops, the nearly vertical potato cliffs that were 10-15 feet high, or sometimes higher, had to be descended together. These sharp drops were usually never more than two body lengths. But if Bic's hand slipped, Polly would drop and be seriously injured. Then both of them would be hobbling along, trying uselessly to get away from Amadeus and his rifle.

"Ready?" Bic asked. "Try not to step on my face this time, okay? Or pull my hair out again. That hurt last time."

"I'll try. No promises," Polly said. Then she began to climb over top of him, exposing herself. Bic was too busy concentrating on not dropping her to enjoy the view. He would never purposely let her fall, but the constant shouting from Amadeus—and now Polly, as she was dangling over a cliff—was rattling his concentration.

"BIC!"

Polly's hand slipped.

"Polly!" Bic closed his eyes and hoped for the best.

Polly hit the ground, hard. Some of the impact was absorbed by the moderately soft potato landing—some, but not all. She landed awkward, then flipped backwards, rolling onto her shoulder. Surprising even herself, she remained mostly uninjured. Bruised and embarrassed, but otherwise just fine.

"I'm okay!" Polly said, slow to her feet. "If you hang over the edge, Bic, I'll try to catch you on the way down. Or at least slow you down. Just try not to—"

A shout interrupted her.

"I KNOW YOU TWO ARE CLOSE!" Amadeus hollered.

Judging by how clear and loud his voice was, he was no more than thirty or forty steps behind them. Perhaps as close as the patch of trees they just ran through.

Polly and Bic locked eyes.

In a panic, Bic swung his body over the ledge, then let go too soon. He dropped nearly three body lengths. His landing was far more uncoordinated than Polly's. The brunt of the impact was taken by his ankle.

"That didn't work." Bic laid still with his eyes closed.

"Bic?" Polly asked, leaning over him. "Are you broken?" She was scared to know the answer, but more frightened of who was right behind them.

"No, nothing broken," Bic said, rubbing his left ankle. "I landed on the same ankle, though. I don't think I can walk on it." The bruise was taking on a dark, purplish hue. And the massive swelling gave the injury a grotesque appearance.

Polly had never seen anyone injured this bad before. She wanted to help, but couldn't.

Scuffling sounds from above drew their attention.

They'd already stayed in one place too long.

When they both looked up, two large potato skin sandals dangled over the ledge they'd just dropped from.

"Hello, children," said Amadeus.

Amadeus aimed the rifle at Bic's skull.

Bic closed his eyes.

100

The rifle clicked.

101

"Hmm." Amadeus peered down into the barrel of the weapon. He shook it. Then he checked the chamber to make sure the rifle was loaded.

"Sorry about that, kids," Amadeus said, apologizing to his close-range targets. "I must've forgot to reload since the last time I tried to shoot you. Wait just one moment, please."

Polly and Bic did not wait just one moment.

They fled.

"Hey, stop!" Amadeus hollered. The pleasant smile never left his heavily-bearded face. He acted as if his killing them was done as a favor.

"Just stay where you are so I can have a good shot! What do you say?" Amadeus hollered. "Then we can stop all this chasing and running. My legs are getting tired."

102

With Polly helping him along, Bic was able weave through the patches of trees, climb over obstacles, and focus on getting away from the madman trying to end both of their lives.

All the continuous movement of Bic's injured ankle minimized the pain, or possibly numbed it so that he could keep on running. But they had to take many short breaks, each one more dangerous than the last, as they sensed that Amadeus was closing in on them.

"Need a rest?" Polly asked when Bic pulled on her arm and forced them to stop.

"No," Bic said, panting. "Go that...that way. Not as steep."

They took off again in the direction Bic suggested. Up until he became hurt, Bic was always getting annoyed with Polly for choosing the path that looked the easiest. Now he was the one choosing the path that looked less hazardous.

It proved to be their one correct guess.

Hardly a few hundred feet away, around one last corner, then down a long but only moderately steep hill, was something else the two of them had only ever seen inside Old Earth magazines.

Grass.

103

Months ago, when the Three Elders had first become suspicious of Jack of Hearts, a most trusted and loyal employee, Amadeus had been sent in as a spy.

The young and impressionable Amadeus, who was always happy to cut corners, downplay other diggers' achievements, or even claim them as his own, was quickly rising in the ranks of digging. Not for his intellect, but merely for his incredible strength and terrific work ethic.

That is why the Three Elders selected Amadeus to be transferred from his own small digging crew to Jack of Hearts' crew, the largest in Yam Hill. This lateral move was done under the guise that Amadeus would eventually be a suitable replacement for Jack of Hearts, the Chief Digger of Yam Hill, while Jack of Hearts himself would be promoted, and possibly voted in as the fourth Elder.

Another Elder lie.

Polly and Bic were now outside the realm where the Three Elders could control them, or stamp them out, or stop them from infecting people with the truth.

Polly assumed the Three Elders were worried that she and Bic would somehow get back inside Yam Hill, explain to the other residents what had happened—not only to them, but also about the illegal Ejection of Jack of Hearts, an extremely well-liked potato resident—and thereby start a revolution.

She was exactly right.

That was precisely the Three Elders' greatest fear. The truth, if exposed, would ruin their way of life.

Since Amadeus had no wife, no children, and had a general dislike for all potato residents, he was precisely the right man for the job. He was a near-perfect personality match for a Solitaire, the loneliest and all-but-forgotten residents of Yam Hill, who usually ended up taking their own potato lives. But Amadeus had never once considered self-Ejection, or ending his own life.

Just the lives of others.

104

Old Earth identifiers such as VIP, CEO, and VP no longer held any credibility. These once hailed acronyms no longer existed, and were not fully understood by the people of Yam Hill.

Any persons of national or international celebrity were dead and gone. No one of any power, perceived or otherwise, survived the Great Unexpected Tragedy.

All but the fifty-seven people saved by the great Mr. Yamhill were lost during the Great Unexpected Tragedy, which raged across the entire planet. The event decimated the human population, leaving only a small percentage of humans left—in Idaho.

Within a single generation, certain people of Yam Hill went right back to the ways of Old Earth, where power was entrusted to a few, instead of belonging to the people.

Corruption and greed, two inescapable features of Old Earth, filtered right through the thick yam walls of Yam Hill.

Inside Yam Hill, Elders had power. And that power was always passed down from generation to generation, from father to son, and so on through the years.

When an Elder calls your name, whether at a Community Meeting or simply in passing, you immediately stop whatever it is you are doing. You listen carefully to what he had to say, and you did not interrupt.

That also goes for anyone employed by the Elders, since they are a representative of the Elders. All residents, young or old, must obey all laws, rules, and even the advice given by either an Elder, or anyone employed by the Elders. Those who do not obey are punished. But sometimes an employee of the Elders takes things too far.

"STOP!" Amadeus shouted, closing in on Polly and Bic. "Why can't you two just die properly? I'm trying to help you!"

When he wasn't yelling at them, demanding they stop and take a bullet each, he would sometimes even beg them to stop. He was a large, strong man, but he was running out of energy, and patience.

"Keep going!" Bic whispered, urging Polly to go on ahead of him. "I'll keep up, I promise."

Though their names were being called, often shouted by an employee of the Three Elders, Polly and Bic did not obey. They did not listen. They ran, and ran, and did not stop running until they reached the bottom of Yam Hill.

105

All residents of Yam Hill believed that Old Earth was uninhabitable. That it was utterly useless for anything other than to warn future potato generations about the dangers of attempting to leave the inner sanctity of the giant yam.

All residents believed this. And they believed it whole-heartedly because the trusted Three Elders told them, always reminding residents that life inside Yam Hill was the only way to survive. There was never any reason to question what an Elder had to say. The Three Elders were the most respected, most loved residents in all of Yam Hill.

They would never lie to anyone.

The very idea was absurd.

Elders were originally put in charge by the founding members of Yam Hill, to take care of everyone, to look after the needs of every single person, no matter how useful, or otherwise.

Things deteriorated rapidly.

Years later, the Elders were still in charge, though not necessarily to take care of residents. Most residents could take care of themselves, with adequate shelter carved out by their own hands, and an everlasting food supply within arm's length.

Instead, the role of the Elders quickly became hiding the truth, keeping everyone...not in the dark, but certainly kept in the dim LED glow of their simple lives.

"Life must continue," the Elders would often say. "Marriages must be formed. Children must be born."

Even the Elders didn't know what might be lying-in-wait outside of Yam Hill. There was only one man who had a decent knowledge about what was happening on Old Earth.

Outside, things had changed.

106

Since so-called "gravity" affected all living things, not just humans, all manner of land and sea animals became extinct in a matter of hours, some in mere minutes.

Animals that were underground, in their burrows or tunnels, or even in caves, survived for a length of time. But same as humans, if they dared to come out into the open, they would've lost their footing immediately, then floated up into the atmosphere. Their bodies would first freeze to death in the troposphere, the lowest level, then burn up and disintegrate while travelling through the extreme high temperatures of the outer atmosphere.

Nearly the entire animal population, creatures large and small, died out during the first twenty-four hours following the Great Unexpected Tragedy.

Surprisingly, in terms of survival and willingness to carry on, or possibly out of sheer stubbornness and refusal to die, the animal population outlasted most of the human population.

107

When least expected, Polly and Bic reached the bottom, where Yam Hill attached to Old Earth.

108

There was a house.
Just like from the Old Earth magazines.

109

Looking up, only now were Polly and Bic able to witness the incredible size of Yam Hill. Taking a few steps back, the giant yam was still too incredibly large to take in from their low viewpoint. All they could see was layer after layer of potato, and tall trees. Some of which were three, four, even five or six times the size of even the largest man inside Yam Hill.

"I think Yam Hill is touching the clouds up there," Bic said, craning his neck to see better. Although they were still being tracked by a madman, a lunatic that wanted to relieve them of the responsibility of living and breathing, this was by far the most incredible sight either of them had ever seen.

"POLLY! BIC!" Amadeus hollered. Then came another blast of the rifle.

Polly and Bic stepped away from the incredible sight of Yam Hill, then hurried around the corner. Neither one cared which direction they went, as long as it was far away from the man trying to shoot them. The man's threats never ceased.

"What is he yelling at us?" Bic asked as they hurried along the outer edges of Yam Hill.

"Probably another threat to kill us," Polly said. She stopped when Bic moaned in pain about his ankle. "You okay? Do we need to stop?"

"No, let's keep going." Bic ignored the pain in his throbbing ankle and continued to walk. "We have to get away. I don't want to stop until we can't hear that man's voice anymore."

For almost an hour they walked.

Both of them were desperately thirsty. And they were both experiencing severe hunger pains. If the chase didn't end soon, their bodies would fail. Then they might as might just give up and hand themselves over to Amadeus.

"Thanks for not leaving me behind," Bic said as he hobbled along with Polly's help. He could walk on his own, but that would've slowed them down. "That Amadeus man would've ended my life by now if you weren't here to help me."

Polly wanted to laugh. "I'm not going to give up on you, Bic. Annoying as you are sometimes, you're still worth saving." Then, unable to resist, she said, "But if you injure your other ankle, then I'll have no choice but to go on without you."

"Funny," Bic said with a grin.

Now that they'd reached the bottom, their troubles had not ceased. If anything, they'd gotten worse. They were still lost. Still tired. Still hungry and scared. And worst of all, still dangerously close to being caught and killed in a gruesome manner, by the rifle—or bare hands—of Amadeus.

Jack of Hearts told them to get to the bottom. That was what he'd shouted, several times. Then, as he was being illegally Ejected, he screamed at them to 'find the yellow house.'

In what direction? Polly wondered.

Bic was looking down as he walked, so didn't see it.

Polly stopped and nearly caused Bic to fall over.

"What's wrong?" Bic feared the worst, seeing his best friend turn rigid. Her eyes were wide with concern, as if she were in pain.

Bic was wrong. She wasn't in pain. Polly had found what they were looking for.

It was the yellow house that Jack of Hearts spoke of. Only it was more of a faded blue color.

110

"Bic, look!" Polly thought it was just another part of Yam Hill. After realizing what it was, her immediate reaction was to recoil, thinking that something, or someone, might come out of the Old Earth entryway, and possibly attack them.

It was a door.

"Do we go in?" Polly asked.

Walking hand in hand, with Polly continuing to aid Bic as his limp became steadily worse, they stood in front of the rectangular section of wood.

Bic reached out a hand, but Polly grabbed him.

"Are you sure? What if it's deception?" Polly was more nervous than Bic. "What if that Amadeus man was leading us here? What is he wants us to go in there, so he can end our lives?"

Polly's senses told her that something behind this Old Earth door was waiting for them. Though what it could possibly be, she had no idea.

Up until this point, doors—especially doors attached to Old Earth houses, like this one—had only been seen in old magazines, or mentioned in books. Behind this door could be something even more frightful than what Amadeus intended for them.

Bic hesitated, but saw no other alternative.

"I don't think we have a choice, Polly," Bic said. "That Amadeus man will find us soon. If not today, then tomorrow or the next day. He'll never give up. Maybe we can hide inside this Old Earth house?"

Polly looked mad. "Bic, I don't think hiding will solve our problem. Amadeus has spent the last two lights and two darks tracking us down. I was thinking there might be something inside, some kind of weapon we could use to..."

Polly choked up.

One word, a particularly difficult word, had failed her, as if her tongue refused to speak it out loud. She knew precisely which word she'd intended to use, but had a hard time saying it. It was not a common word inside Yam Hill. Not all residents knew what the word truly meant.

"Kill him?" Bic suggested, knowing exactly what Polly meant to say.

The word "kill" was tough to hear. But it was a choice they would have to make, or else the choice would be made for them. And they would be on the receiving end of an Old Earth rifle, instead of what Polly was suggesting.

"Someone has to shoot him, Bic," Polly said. "If we don't do it, then he will absolutely do it to us. He won't stop until we're dead, Bic."

More shouting behind them.

Amadeus was near.

"What are those?" Polly pointed high over their heads, distracted by the glare. Maybe eight or ten feet above their heads, were several shiny rectangles, all made of something unlike the rest of the house. They were repelling the bright light from the sun, making them hard to look at, but fascinating to see.

"I think those are..." Bic had to think hard to remember the right word, but he could only think of words such as sea, and ocean, and glass.

"Windows?" Polly suggested.

"Yes!" Bic was thinking of something else entirely. "I think that's what people of Old Earth called them. They were used for..." Bic shook his head, disappointed that he couldn't remember. "I don't exactly know what windows are for."

"Look!" Polly pointed to the window.

Bic looked up and saw it, too. There was a shape, perhaps a resident of Yam Hill, standing somehow behind the Old Earth window. By the time he shielded his eyes from the sunlight, shining directly behind them, the figure was gone.

Shouts, again.

This time much closer.

Hardly a moment before, the threats had been indiscernible, obviously being shouted in vain, and from a reasonably safe distance. Now Amadeus sounded close enough that he might suddenly appear around the corner. Then both Bic and Polly's life would be over with one, perhaps two or three loud blasts of the rifle.

Together, Polly and Bic pushed on the door.

"Hm."

The door didn't move.

"I think..." Bic steadied himself using Polly's shoulder. He hobbled closer to the door, then reached out a hand to grab a hold of the round, gold-colored object attached to roughly the middle of the Old Earth door.

Bic pulled, pushed, then finally twisted the shiny round object—what was referred to in the days of Old Earth as a door knob. And it worked.

With the slightest push, the door swung open.

This was followed by another surprise. The owner of the house was standing there, waiting to greet them both.

"Hello, Polly. Hello, Bic."

III

While the Great Unexpected Tragedy was still happening all across the world, as well as in Idaho, Mr. Yamhill's possessions—the contents of his entire house, from the very light to the extremely heavy—were all floating around the house.

Including Mr. Yamhill.

When everything came back down again, much of it was destroyed. Everything that was not made of glass and could be salvaged, the furniture, books, pictures, all his durable keepsakes, were all put back in relatively the same spot, hung back up on the walls, or pieced back together again.

The chaos and floating disorder that he had lived in for several days before the yam swallowed up his home, his shed, and the surrounding land, was eventually put right again. Everything was put back together in relatively the same way that the Yamhill's (including Mrs. Yamhill, when she was alive) had kept things for their nearly forty-two years together.

This was exactly how Polly and Bic found it.

Waiting to greet them was the First Elder.

In this new light, the sunlight—not the dim red LED glow of the interior of Yam Hill—he was still a large man. Only now he didn't seem so overwhelming and powerful. Here, he looked more like everyone else, except for the nicely trimmed beard, the combed hair, and his colorful body covering.

Polly immediately noticed his strange clothes.

The garments worn by the First Elder were much more form-fitting, more human-shaped, with a spot for each arm and each leg to fit nicely into. His body covering was much different than what Polly and Bic (and every other resident of Yam Hill) wore everyday: thick, uncomfortable potato skin.

"This is Mr. Yamhill's house, isn't it?" Bic said, as if encountering the First Elder was of no significance. More than anything, he was in awe of where he was standing in: the living room of the creator of Yam Hill. Looking around the room, Bic's mind filled with wonder and delight.

"Yes, Bic, it is," said the First Elder. "You are absolutely correct. This house once belonged to Mr. Raymond Yamhill, the creator of our beloved potato. And his wife, Betty, when she was alive."

"There's so much to look at!" Bic began to explore the room further, completely oblivious to their dangerous situation. Not only having the First Elder to deal with, but with Amadeus still hunting them down. He couldn't help but be absolutely fascinated by the rows of books. All of them were lined on a tall, rectangular device made of wood—what people of the Old Earth called a bookshelf. Several more books were open, lying on top of the odd-shaped table, with its smooth brown surface and pointed corners.

"Polly, look at all this!" Bic stared with huge eyes at some of the art work hanging on the walls. Even the walls themselves were impressive, so perfectly flat, unlike the wavy and slanted potato walls inside Yam Hill.

Polly was not impressed. She was too mad, or perhaps too frightened of the First Elder to enjoy all there was to see inside the house of Mr. Yamhill.

Polly stepped forward. "So what are you doing here, Elder?"

Instead of getting mad, the First Elder smiled.

Polly drew back. She couldn't believe she was being smiled at by the man who had Ejected her. By the same man who had dragged her by the wrist, and her hair, halfway across Yam Hill, up the 2,080 potato steps to the Ejection site, and then with hardly more than a dozen words, had pushed her out the small Ejection hole carved into the side.

That same man was now looking at her with something close to empathy, even compassion.

"I live here, Polly," said the First Elder. "We all do, the other Elders and myself. All other residents are not permitted inside the house, of course. Not even to visit.

Although that was permitted in the past, the current Elders do not allow it. Residents live in their yam homes, and we live here."

"In all this fancy, bright light? With all this room? And all these…*things* to look at?" Polly was so mad she could hardly get her words out. She was trembling, ready to lash out at the First Elder.

While Bic was busy flipping through the pages of a colorful book, Polly was scanning the room for something she could use as a weapon. Something to harm the First Elder with, or at least protect herself whenever he tried to grab her again.

Bic was too enthralled with all the pictures, and paintings, and all sorts of other fancy objects to pay attention to what was really happening.

Truth, revealed.

Lies, exposed.

Polly assumed that Bic mistakenly felt safe now that the First Elder was with them. As if this horrible man would protect them from Amadeus, who was probably near the house by now. The next time they met, she knew the dangerous man would not forget to reload his rifle.

"So you three, all the Elders, spend your whole life inside Mr. Yamhill's home," Polly said in a raised voice and pointing a finger, "with all these books and paintings, and all this bright sunlight to see, with stars and trees to look at outside, while everyone else lives inside a giant potato? In the dark?"

"Yes."

Polly crossed her arms, attempting to cover up her nearly exposed chest. With all the slipping and sliding down edges and cliffs, desperately trying to get away from a killer, her potato skin covering had torn in several spots. She would need a new potato covering if life outside Yam Hill was to continue. The First Elder had seen to it that her life inside Yam Hill was over, so why would he allow her to live outside?

"If you will calm down, Polly," said the First Elder, "and let me explain a few things, then I can probably answer all of your—"

That's as far as he got.

Polly delivered an angry speech, full of hateful language, drumming up every awful word she could think of. She didn't know many, since the books that residents of Yam Hill were given to read were essentially void of foul language and offensive words.

Most of her speech was extremely unkind, and directed specifically at the First Elder. Polly went on for so long that her voice began to fail.

"Polly? If you will listen for a moment," said the First Elder, "I will explain. Or at least try to explain, as best I can. But you won't let me get in a word."

Polly wanted no part of his explanation.

"Polly?" The First Elder's loud voice was soft today.

"What?"

The First Elder was being extremely patient with her. "If you won't listen to me, Polly, then will you perhaps listen to someone else?"

Without any further explanation, the First Elder called out to someone in another room. His loud voice echoed throughout the house, easily heard by anyone in the vicinity.

"I'm on my way!" said a familiar voice.

A woman stepped into the room.

This familiar lady looked even prettier in the Old Earth sunlight coming in through the window. Her stomach was very round, as she was within just a couple weeks, or perhaps only a few of days of brining a new child into Yam Hill.

112

Old Earth's population, at one time, was over seven billion. All those children were born in precisely the same manner that children of Yam Hill were born.

Hospitals were still a relatively young invention, as far as Old Earth was concerned.

Centuries ago, even thousands of years ago, children came into the world without much more than a few people nearby, friends or family—usually other women—to guard over the new mother in case anything went wrong. There were no electric monitors, no trained doctors and nurses, and certainly no vaccinations.

Children found a way to survive.

Not all, but most.

113

Many years ago, the Elders devised a plan. The idea was to select a woman—or two, or even three, if more than one was available—who would be a mother to all children of Yam Hill.

The woman (or women) had to be of the proper age, unmarried, and would have to volunteer for the position to be a Mother of Yam Hill.

She would have many children.

As many as she could, to prolong life in Yam Hill.

114

By a vote of 2-1, Polly had been selected.
Polly would become a Mother of Yam Hill.

115

During the days of Old Earth, it was estimated that close to 350,000 children were born every single day.

It was also estimated that close to 150,000 people died every single day.

116

"Ms. Doppelganger?" Polly said. "Why are you here? Are you with him? Please don't tell me that you're a part of this. You're one of the people I trust the most."

Into the room came sweet old Ms. Doppelganger, walking slow and deliberate, taking care not to slip and injure herself, or the child inside her.

Polly hardly recognized her old friend.

Today she was wearing body coverings similar to what the First Elder was wearing. Only instead of two separate leg coverings, hers only had one, which fitted both legs. It was some kind of thin body covering, with beautiful patterns and Old Earth flowers printed all over it.

Not only Ms. Doppelganger's clothes, but her entire appearance was different. Her face was pretty, much more than usual. Something was painted on her lips, her cheeks, even above her eyes.

Bic turned around to greet her. "Hello, Ms. Doppelganger."

"Hello, Bic," said a cheerful Ms. Doppelganger. "I'm so glad you two made it."

"Have you seen this book?" Bic asked her. "This is amazing!"

Ms. Doppelganger smiled. "Yes, I have looked through that particular book, Bic. It's an absolute wonder what those artists were capable of."

Polly was ready to fall apart.

"Hello, my beautiful Polly," said Ms. Doppelganger, turning her attention to the young lady standing in front of her. "We were worried about you. There are a lot of dangers out there." She pointed out the window, indicating Old Earth.

"Many unknown dangers," the First Elder added.

"Yes, especially with that lunatic, Amadeus, chasing after them," said Ms. Doppelganger, cringing. "I never did like that young man. I knew right from the start that there was something odd about him. But Jack of Hearts always took such excellent care of you, Polly, didn't he?"

"As did her daily parents," said the First Elder.

"My daily parents?" Polly suddenly felt the need to sit down instead of fight.

Bic looked up from his book. "He's talking about your non-true mother and father. The ones who raised you." He shook his head and added, "I never did think that Polly looked like either of her parents. I always thought Polly looked more like—well, you know who I mean." His eyes darted between the First Elder and Polly, then he quickly looked away.

"Jack of Hearts?" suggested the First Elder.

Bic went back to reading his book. He looked completely relaxed, as if he was at home in his bedroom, and everything was fine.

Everything was not fine.

"Ms. D—?" Polly could hardly speak. And her body was in great danger of crashing to the strange, smooth floor made of hard wood.

"Elder, will you?" Ms. Doppelganger held out one arm at the elbow, which the First Elder immediately took and helped her to sit on the strange, cushioned furniture. Then Ms. Doppelganger gestured for Polly to sit down beside her.

Polly took the offer and sat down. She needed answers to questions that she couldn't even think up. Too much was happening, too fast—the complete opposite of normal life inside Yam Hill.

"Well, first off, you're safe," said Ms. Doppelganger, then she patted Polly's leg. "You're safe, Polly. No one will harm you in here. That much, I promise."

Polly's tears finally released. Not because she felt safe, not at all, but because her head began to hurt from trying to figure this all out.

"As you can see..." Ms. Doppelganger took a moment to move herself back on the Old Earth furniture, trying to get comfortable. "Oh, that's better. I am about to have another child, Polly."

Polly wiped her tears away, then held out a hand to touch the tiny child growing inside Ms. Doppelganger. She needed something to take her mind off all the questions. And a new child was always something special to appreciate.

"It's perfectly all right, Polly," said Ms. Doppelganger. "You may, child, go ahead."

Polly gently placed her hand on Ms. Doppelganger's midsection. Her stomach was round and hard in spots, soft and curved in others. Only one other time had Polly had the opportunity to touch and feel the stomach of a woman who was about to bring a new child into Yam Hill. It was a lady down the hallway from Polly's ex-home, a friend of her mother's. That time, the child must've been sleeping inside, so she didn't get to feel the child kick or move. But when Polly placed her hand this time, right on the highest part of Ms. Doppelganger's round stomach, the child moved.

Polly smiled so big her lips cracked.

"How many children is it now, Ms. Doppelganger?" asked the First Elder.

"This makes eleven," Ms. Doppelganger answered. "Not including the mishaps. And two of them are *yours*, Elder. Just in case you need reminding." Then she gave him a look and a playful smile.

"I haven't forgotten, Marlene," said the First Elder, returning the playful smile. "Not when you remind me every chance you get."

Polly couldn't believe these two. After all she and Bic had been through, here they were acting like friends, perhaps even more. But after thinking about Ms. Doppelganger's situation, how she was about to create a new child, perhaps she was going through more than even Polly and Bic had these last few days.

"Why don't you do something useful this morning," Ms. Doppelganger said to the First Elder, "and get these two a drink of water. They must both be terribly thirty. Polly's lips are so chapped they're bleeding."

The First Elder left their room for another, disappearing around a perfectly sculpted and vertical wall. Around the corner, Polly heard noises like she'd never heard before. The First Elder came back into the room holding two strange, circular objects. Inside was a clear, sloshing liquid. One glass was given to Polly, the other to Bic.

"Water?" Bic looked at this new drink with fascinated eyes. "Polly, you can see through it!" With one hand, he balanced his heavy book on his hip, and the other hand to hold his drink. He held up his glass of water, studying it. He smelled it, then drank some.

"It's so...soft." Bic was surprised how easy it was to swallow. It was much different, much thinner, with a less gritty taste than potato juice, the only available liquid inside Yam Hill.

"Go ahead, Polly," said the First Elder. "I promise, it's the same as the Elders and I drink. The same as Ms. Doppelganger, and all the other Mothers of Yam Hill drink during the months of carrying a new potato child."

"It's good, Polly," Bic said. "Try it."

Polly took her first drink of pure water.

"Thank you, Quinton," said Ms. Doppelganger, though at first Polly had no idea who she was talking to.

"Quinton," Polly asked, confused.

The First Elder nodded. "Yes, Polly. My Old Earth name was Quinton Parks. I was nineteen years old when Mr. Yamhill rescued me. He came walking right up to the front door of my house, wearing those strange boots of his. Those incredible, life-saving boots that allowed him to rescue me, plus fifty-six other people, and bring us into the safe environment of Yam Hill."

The room became quiet.

"Wait. What?" Polly had to think. "You mean...you were alive back then? During the Great Unexpected Tragedy?"

"Yes, Polly." The First Elder looked her right in the eye, speaking the truth. "In fact, I am the last living survivor of the Great Unexpected Tragedy."

Polly didn't believe it. "That can't be right."

"It's all true, Polly," said Ms. Doppelganger. "Quinton really was rescued by Mr. Yamhill nearly half a century ago. I wasn't there during the Great Unexpected Tragedy—thank goodness. But I was one of the first children born inside Yam Hill."

Polly's head began to hurt. She looked back and forth between the First Elder and Ms. Doppelganger, trying to decide if they were telling the truth.

Apparently, they were.

"So, if you were nineteen when you were rescued, that means now you're..." Polly did some quick counting in her head, but Bic beat him to it.

"Seventy years old?" Bic suggested.

"Yes, almost," said the First Elder with a smile. "I will be seventy years old next year, Bic. And next year marks the fiftieth anniversary of Yam Hill. Fifty years of living inside this safe, crime-free, disease-free, food and shelter providing potato we call home."

"So..." Bic looked puzzled.

"Go ahead, Bic," said the First Elder. "You may ask me anything you like. I will try to answer it as best I can."

Bic worked up the courage to ask: "Is your name really Quinton?"

Polly scoffed at him. "Bic? Is that really all you want to know? After all we've been through, you ask him about his name?"

"I was just wondering," Bic said, sounding hurt.

Polly wanted to laugh, but didn't have the energy. She found it incredible that her friend's mind was somewhere else, probably lost in the book he was holding, from Old Earth, which turned out not to be so old after all.

"Yes, Bic, I promise that is really and truly my first name," said the First Elder. "I can assure you that I am the only 'Quinton' living inside Yam Hill. Names have always been tricky, especially with all the new parents."

"Don't I know it," said Ms. Doppelganger, adjusting herself on the seat. "Here I am, about to pop, and the Second Elder hasn't even come close to deciding on a name, whether a boy or girl."

Polly's hand recoiled, only slightly, when she realized it was the Second Elder's child. She put it back, and almost instantly felt a tiny kick.

"When I first became an Elder, nearly forty years ago," the First Elder went on, "every new mother wanted to call their child Raymond, named after Mr. Raymond Yamhill. But with so many *Raymonds* being born, especially when several lived in the same area of Yam Hill, it became quite confusing. That is why the Elders, past and present, choose the names of all the children born into Yam Hill. The new parents always have some input when choosing the name for their child, whether their true child or not. But the Elders and I work hard to provide new names to be used. Names that will not be so easily confused."

"Like my name, Bic Lighter." Bic had already finished off his glass of water, then placed his empty glass on the large wooden rectangle holding all the books.

"Correct, Bic," said the First Elder.

"But you told me a few years ago," Bic continued, "that my name shouldn't have been accepted because my name means fire."

"Yes, that is also true, Bic," said the First Elder. He took a seat on the soft rectangle furniture, directly across from Polly and Ms. Doppelganger. "I tried to explain to your parents the history of your name, and what a 'Bic Lighter' actually was during the days of Old Earth, but your parents—young as they were when they had you—were absolutely determined that was to be your name. And besides, that name—"

"—fits him perfectly," interrupted Ms. Doppelganger, and she smiled at Bic.

Polly looked at the First Elder. "What about my name?"

"Polly Want a Cracker?" The First Elder looked thoughtfully at the angry young woman sitting across from him, holding onto Ms. Doppelganger's hand.

Ms. Doppelganger said, "Tell her the truth, Quinton."

The First Elder agreed that he would.

"Your true father chose that name for you, Polly," the First Elder explained. "At the time you were born, 'Polly' was a name the Elders and I suggested during a Community Meeting. Of course, several women immediately chose that name for their upcoming child. But Jack of Hearts wanted to avoid confusion with the other girls born with the same name. He, too, was expecting a child—you, Polly."

Polly listened, for once, without interruption.

"When you were born, Jack of Hearts, along with your true mother, had no idea if you were going to be a girl."

"If you were to be born a boy," said Ms. Doppelganger, "Jack of Hearts was still clueless as to what he was going to name you. Right up until the day you came into Yam Hill, he still hadn't decided on a boy's name. He was so thrilled that you were born a girl."

The First Elder smiled. "Your name was selected from the pages of a book on the shelf over there," said the First Elder, and pointed to where Bic was standing. "Treasure Island is the name of the book. I believe Jack of Hearts has our only copy right now."

"It's about the only book he ever reads," said Ms. Doppelganger. "Over and over again, front to back. He keeps it with him at all times out there."

Ms. Doppelganger meant Old Earth.

"Yes, my Jack often reads that book when he's out on a mission, or on a hunting trip for us," said the First Elder. "He says it's because it reminds him of you, Polly."

"What about the other girls?" Polly asked. "I've travelled all over Yam Hill and I've never met anyone else with my name."

"Yes," the First Elder said with a laugh. "You certainly have travelled quite extensively. All throughout Yam Hill, since you were quite young. If my memory is still in proper working order, I would say that you, Polly, did even more travelling throughout your childhood than even Jack of Hearts did."

All this talking about Jack of Hearts, her true father, made her miss him even more.

"To answer your question, Polly," the First Elder went on, "the other girls—the other Polly's, that is—no longer exist. Two sets of parents decided to change the name of their child soon after its arrival. And the third one simply failed to wake up one morning."

"She died?" Polly asked.

The First Elder nodded.

"That's sad," Bic said with his nose still buried in the book, but paying at least partial attention to the conversation.

"As Bic already mentioned earlier," said the First Elder, "there is a resemblance between you and Jack of Hearts for a reason, Polly."

"Yes, we know about that already, Elder," Bic said. "We read about it in the letter. Jack of Hearts is Polly's true father."

Mrs. Doppelganger patted Polly's leg and gave her hand a gentle squeeze. "I'm glad, Polly. I'm glad that you finally know the truth about your father. For so long we wanted to tell you, but we simply couldn't."

Polly ripped her hand away from Ms. Doppelganger. "You knew that Jack of Hearts was my true father and didn't tell me?" Polly's accusing face nearly brought Ms. Doppelganger to tears.

"How could you keep that from me?" Polly went on. "I thought you were a true friend. But now I find out that you were lying to me all along."

Polly's voice grew louder, angrier with each declaration, each accusation. She refused to hold the hand of this new deceitful version of Ms. Doppelganger, who up until now had always told her the truth. Now she, too, turned out to be a liar.

"Adults can't be trusted," Polly said, a sharp tone to her voice, pointing at the grownups in the room.

"Polly?" The First Elder tried to intervene.

"All these years I've known you, Ms. D," Polly went on, "all those long talks we had, all those visits, and you never once even gave me any hint who my true father was. How could you lie to me?"

"Polly," said the First Elder, more forcefully.

"You're no better than *him*." Polly flicked a finger towards the First Elder. Turning away, she folded her arms across her chest and sank back as far as she could. "You're just another liar."

"POLLY!" The First Elder's voice was so loud this time that Polly shrunk away from it, even further into the soft furniture.

After a short silence, when it was clear that Polly was not going to interrupt again, the First Elder told Polly something she always felt in her heart was true, but never dared questioned the people who had raised her.

"Ms. Doppelganger is not a liar," said the First Elder. "She is your mother, Polly. Your true mother."

117

After an hour of talking, of sharing explanations, and accepting apologies, most of Polly's questions were answered. Surprising even herself, she became less and less hostile towards the First Elder.

With so much new information to process, Polly and Bic had forgotten about Amadeus, who was still out there.

Bic drank three more glasses of water.

Polly was on her fourth glass.

118

Life on Old Earth sounded strange.
Life in Yam Hill sounded quite reasonable.

119

Bic found out that the two people who had raised him since the day he came into Yam Hill, were his true mother and true father.

What he was not prepared for was that he had already been replaced with a new potato child.

Bic was now sitting beside Polly, draped over the side of the Old Earth seat, groaning in self-pity. When he found out that there was someone else living with his family—his old family, living in his old room—he was not so enthralled with the art book anymore.

"I can't believe they've forgotten about me already," Bic said, sulking with his head in his hands.

"Your mother and father have not forgotten about you, Bic," said the First Elder. "I was there just yesterday. They still speak very highly of you. But they had to be told the truth about what happened, and where you were."

"You mean part of the truth," Polly said. "Not all."

"Yes, Polly. Both of your parents—yours and Bic's— were given reasonable answers as to why neither of you would be returning," said the First Elder. "After your false Ejection—"

"Our real Ejection, you mean," Polly interrupted again, though not nearly as impolitely as she'd done over the past hour.

The First Elder did not get mad, but smiled. "We've already been through that, Polly. It was a false Ejection, made to look real for the purpose of fooling not only the Second and Third Elder, but also Amadeus."

Ms. Doppelganger cringed at the name.

"I don't know what it is about that young man," said Ms. Doppelganger. "I'm certainly glad he is no child of mine. Imagine actually taking it upon himself to set off after two innocent children in hopes of…well, you can imagine what he's capable of…" She couldn't stand to say the word "kill" either.

The First Elder also looked concerned, even worried about the man's capabilities.

"And why? All for the sole purpose of trying to impress the other two Elders," Ms. Doppelganger went on, not ashamed in the least for expressing her anger. "The only thing that impresses those two is every time Jack of Hearts prepares a feast."

Polly and Bic both enjoyed listening, especially when the conversation between the two adults in the room spoke with passion in their voices. Polly had never heard sweet old Ms. Doppelganger sound so irate, so intense. She may be small, shorter than Polly, but she was passionate and strong-minded. After eleven children, she was as tough as a woman could be.

Ms. Doppelganger and the First Elder spoke a long time, while Polly and Bic tried to follow along.

At one point, Polly's mind momentarily slipped away from the conversation, thinking about how much love she felt towards her mother—her true mother. She'd always wanted to grow up to be like Ms. Doppelganger, even before she knew the truth. Now more than ever, she wanted to grow up to be as strong as her. Especially as she listened to her praise Jack of Hearts, then go on to berate not only Amadeus, but also the other two Elders. If it came down to a choice, even the slightest possibility of a chance, Polly would choose to stay with Ms. Doppelganger forever, until the end of her life.

"Right, Polly?"

The First Elder had spoken her name.

"Hm?" Polly looked up, away from the child growing inside her true mother. She was fascinated by the fact that this new child would be her sister.

"Yes, Elder?"

"Polly, I was just explaining about how Amadeus took it upon himself to chase after you and Bic," explained the First Elder. "As soon as Amadeus and I got back here after your Ejection, the other Elders and I held a meeting. We needed to decide what to say at the Community Meeting, regarding the loss of two young residents. While we were engaged, Amadeus took the rifle and left us a poorly-written note explaining that he, acting alone, was going to crawl outside Jack of Hearts' tunnel, to not only make sure that you two were, in fact, dead, but also that Jack of Hearts was dead."

Ms. Doppelganger led the conversation for a while, wishing to change the subject. She shared stories and talked about Jack of Hearts with kind words, speaking almost as if he was still alive.

Polly loved hearing the First Elder and Ms. Doppelganger talk about her true father, and how much he loved his only daughter.

"So Jack of Hearts—my true father, I mean," Polly said. "He knew about all this? About our Ejection? About Bic and I going outside Yam Hill?"

"Of course he did, Polly," said the First Elder. "Jack of Hearts planned it all. It was all his idea."

Even Bic paid attention after hearing this revelation. After all, he was also a part of the elaborate "escape plan" put together by Jack of Hearts.

"It's true, Polly," said Ms. Doppelganger. "All done in secret, of course. Nothing was ever discussed in front of the Second or Third Elder. Many times, the First Elder and Jack of Hearts would come over to my room, and we would all go over the planning of this. To make sure everything had been accounted for, and that every possible outcome would work in our favor."

"Yes, there were many dozens, if not hundreds of conversations," the First Elder added.

"Jack of Hearts planned the entire event himself," said Ms. Doppelganger. "He would never allow you, or Bic, to be hurt. That's why he did all he could to protect you both during the Ejection process. And still, none of us could foresee what Amadeus would take it upon himself to do…that monster of a man."

Polly and Bic both stiffened.

Amadeus was still out there.

"As I stated earlier," said the First Elder, "none of us anticipated Amadeus taking it upon himself to finalize the plan himself."

Polly had to be satisfied with knowing that Jack of Hearts had planned this wild "escape" for her and Bic, who was sitting close to her, processing his thoughts with a look of total concentration.

It was hard for Polly to deal with the fact that, all this time, the First Elder was not only involved in her escape, but that he wanted to help her.

Jack of Hearts, the First Elder, even Ms. Doppelganger had all worked up this great plan to make sure Polly's family, and Bic's family, all residents of Yam Hill, and especially Amadeus and the Second and Third Elder, all thought she and Bic were dead. Ejected. No longer in existence.

For what reason? Polly wondered.

Why the need to escape?

"So..." Bic was thinking hard. "First Elder, you said a little while ago that you are actually the true father of Jack of Hearts, right?"

"Yes."

"And that Jack of Hearts' true mother died a long time ago, right?"

"Also true," said the First Elder. "Polly's grandmother, a wonderful lady named Iz, short for the Old Earth name Izabella, died shortly after Polly was born."

Polly squeezed Ms. Doppelganger's hand. It was difficult to hear about her grandmother, a woman she never had a chance to meet.

"So that means..." Bic looked at Polly, then back to the First Elder. Unknown to Polly, he was trying to spot the resemblance. Sitting in Mr. Yamhill's living room, with the sunlight pouring in, the resemblance was clearly there—the face, the hair, and especially the eyes.

"Use your words, Bic," Polly said, still not seeing the connection.

Bic looked at Polly, giving her the same type of look that she usually gave him when he couldn't come up with answers fast enough.

"Polly? He's your grandfather," said Bic.

Polly did not shrink back this time.

"Yes, Bic, that is also true," said the First Elder, speaking to Bic but looking directly at Polly. "I assumed that particular subject would've come up at some point during this long conversation. Honestly, I thought that it would've occurred much sooner than—"

The rifle blast outside cut him off.

Amadeus was outside.

120

The First Elder jumped up from the Old Earth couch with surprising speed. Expecting the worst, Polly, Bic and Ms. Doppelganger remained seated. They stayed where they were, watching the First Elder as he stared silently out the window. All of them awaited some kind of instruction from him.

Run?

Hide?

Defend themselves?

"What is it, Quinton?" asked Ms. Doppelganger after a long silence. "What's happening out there? Is it him? Is it Amadeus?"

The First Elder held up a finger, to silence her. For a long time, he did not speak. His silence caused them to worry even more.

"Oh. I see..." The First Elder peered out the living room window, looking down, moving his head side to side to see better. "That's what happens when a bullet strikes a human body. So much blood..."

121

The First Elder had personally witnessed many fights in his nearly seventy years of life. As a teenager living on Old Earth, he had even seen fights on something called television, boxing matches, men and woman fighting in roped off areas.

Inside Yam Hill, he had also been involved in many escalated arguments, even bouts of pushing and shoving in his nearly fifty years of life inside Yam Hill.

Nothing like this battle outside the window.

He caught only the tail end of the fight between the two men outside, grappling, struggling, striking and punishing. Even from his raised viewpoint, standing at the living room window, the First Elder could appreciate the immense power of these two young men, fighting to the death.

One man fell, clearly beaten.

The final rifle blast rattled the window.

122

A large man, dressed in Old Earth hunting clothes with patches of greens and browns, had fatally shot another man.

The face of the attacker was covered, so the First Elder was unable to get a visual identification of the man who was still alive, the clear winner of the battle.

The large man stepped over the body of the deceased, as if the dead body was nothing more than a sack of potatoes.

The attacker headed for the front door.

123

Polly let out a rare scream when the front door violently burst open. A man stood there. He pulled the Old Earth hat from his head to reveal himself.

"Hello, my beautiful Polly," said Jack of Hearts. "Ready to start your new life?"

"Everything will be fine, father," said Jack of Hearts for the third, fourth, possibly fifth or sixth time.

Polly and Bic had already said their goodbyes. Toughest of all, at least for Polly, was saying goodbye to Ms. Doppelganger.

Her mother flat out demanded that her daughter leave, and never return to Yam Hill.

"As much as I want you to stay, Polly, I can't allow it. Neither can your father. He wants to save you from this lifestyle," Ms. Doppelganger said, then pointed to her round belly.

The Second and Third Elder wanted Polly, a pretty young woman who was now the appropriate age, to become a Mother of Yam Hill.

Although the First Elder could have no part, being related to her, the Second and Third Elder had absolutely no connection to Polly.

Polly was ready to leave Yam Hill for good.

Ms. Doppelganger informed her daughter that not only had the other two Elders already picked out Polly's new Mother of Yam Hill name (she would become known as 'Ms. Heart'), they were also having a digging crew carve her out a new potato home. An isolated room, where visits from the Elders would happen frequently, each of them given a block of time for the ritual of natural conception. After those children were born, she would then provide a child for any Elder-selected married couple that wanted a child, but were unable.

Learning all this, the only moderately tempting idea for Polly was the part about all the wonderful Old Earth foods provided only to Mothers of Yam Hill, foods in a can, and something called fresh meat. But Jack of Hearts would teach them all that.

Polly and Bic stood together, waiting patiently while Jack of Hearts said his final goodbye to his true father. Polly squeezed Bic's hand, and he squeezed it back.

The First Elder peered at his son, who was nearly the exact height, perhaps even a bit taller than him.

"Be careful, son."

"I promise, father," said Jack of Hearts. "We will be fine. All of us."

"Yes, I know. Believe me, I know," said the First Elder. "But a father cannot help but to worry about his son. And his granddaughter."

Jack of Hearts smiled rarely. But today was a rare day, and his huge smile took the attention away from his bloodied face, injured from the fight.

"But who better to teach them about the ways of Old Earth than you, my son," said the First Elder. "You've been on hundreds of missions for us over the years, travelling through the wilderness since you were—what, sixteen years old?"

"Fourteen," said Jack of Hearts with a smile. But his smile faded when he turned to the right, indicating the large body of a man, not moving.

Amadeus's body was now covered up with a long section of potato skin.

"Now that he's been taken care of…" Jack of Hearts felt no remorse for what he'd done. "I know that the three of us will be safe out there."

The First Elder nodded. "I will see to it that Amadeus's body is never found. I will tell the other Elders what happened just as soon as they return."

"Thank you."

"No need to thank me, son." With a worried expression as he looked back towards the house, he added, "Which reminds me…they could be back any minute now, so off you go, son. I will do my best to make sure the Second and Third Elder forget all about you. Or at least try to, in order that you three can start your new life together…out there."

Jack of Hearts gave his true father a full-body embrace.

"I know that you and the other two Elders never got along well," said the First Elder, "but I am absolutely certain they will miss all those wonderful feasts you've prepared for us over the years."

Jack of Hearts laughed. "Well, don't worry, Elder. Maybe I'll stop by once in a while and cook a meal for them. And for you."

"You concentrate on your new family. I want you to focus on your new life out there, where anything could happen again. That includes another Great Tragedy."

Jack of Hearts left his father standing at the front entrance to Mr. Yamhill's home, which had to be carved out periodically, since Yam Hill never stopped growing.

Over his shoulder, Jack of Hearts shouted: "I'm certain the other Elders won't be too upset to find out I'm still alive…especially if I bring them some meat once a month."

Jack of Hearts joined up with Polly and Bic, standing on the edge of wilderness—Old Earth.

"I'll also check on the generator every few days, make sure you all have power!" hollered Jack of Hearts. "Goodbye, Ms. D!"

"Goodbye, Jack of Hearts!" called Ms. Doppelganger. "Promise to take care of my little girl! And Bic too, please!"

Jack of Hearts promised he would keep them both safe.

Polly's right hand gripped the left hand of Jack of Hearts. In turn, Jack of Hearts draped his arm over the shoulders of Bic, the future husband of his daughter, selected by him, which he would eventually have to come to terms with.

All three of them prepared their minds for a lifetime about to be spent on Old Earth, as the only free-living people in existence.

In front of them, all around, was once a busy neighborhood, which was now overgrown with trees, and filled with wildlife. It was the old neighborhood of the creator of Yam Hill. For many decades, Mr. Raymond Yamhill's old neighborhood was busy with people and cars, noise and traffic, friends and neighbors. But now, decades after the Great Tragedy, many of those same houses had collapsed, some with massive tall trees growing right through the middle of them.

"Ready for this?" Jack of Hearts asked his daughter.

"No," Polly said, unsure of what her future would be like. But she knew in her heart that with Jack of Hearts alongside them, she and Bic had a much better chance of survival.

Bic turned around and shouted: "Goodbye, Elder! Goodbye, Ms. Doppelganger!"

Polly said the same thing, to each of them, and returned their odd arm movement, the Old Earth custom of waving goodbye. Then she turned around to face her new life.

Life outside Yam Hill.

Soon, the Old Earth would repopulate.

Much the way it did the first time.

With one boy, one girl, and a guide.

Tevin Hansen is the author of numerous books and short stories. He currently resides in Lincoln, Nebraska, where he enjoys skateboarding, reading half a dozen books simultaneously, and chasing his two small children around the house while singing horrendous versions of children's songs.

To find out more go to:
www.handersenpublishing.com
www.tevinhansen.com

Thank you for purchasing and reading Yam Hill.

Handersen Publishing, LLC is an independent publishing house that specializes in creating quality young adult, middle grade, and picture books.

We hope you enjoyed this book and will consider leaving a review on Goodreads or Amazon. A small review can make a big difference for the little guys.

Thank you.

More Books from Handersen Publishing

Also from Handersen Publishing

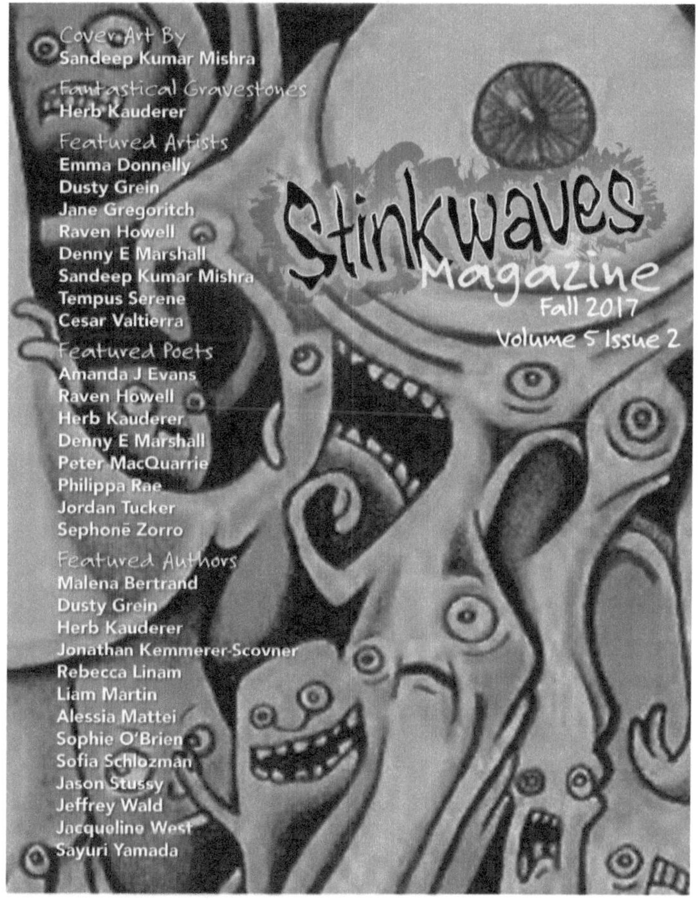

Stinkwaves started in 2013 as a zine, but has now grown into a "mega-zine" filled with the works of talented Indie authors, poets & illustrators. Each issue is packed with short stories, flash fiction, poetry, illustrations, and author interviews.

www.stinkwavesmagazine.com